# Herron Hall

## Claire Bradley

Published by New Generation Publishing in 2022

First Edition

ISBN    978-1-80369-241-8

**www.newgeneration-publishing**

New Generation Publishing

# Chapter 1

Emily was not the sort of woman who was deterred by something so trivial as the weather but as the rain lashed against her face she was regretting making the long trek across London. Thankfully more through luck than foresight, she was sensibly dressed in a thick woollen coat and a hat with a large brim which helped protect her against the elements.

She'd long since given up on her umbrella as it had blown several times inside out and now lay at the bottom of her bag. Emily's legs ached and were not helped by her sodden shoes which squelched with every step she took. Reluctantly she admitted to herself, she felt cold, wet and tired.

It had rained continually throughout most of the day and large puddles had formed on the sides of the pavements. Tonight was not a night to venture outside, in fact it was the sort of evening only to be spent indoors.

Emily and Victoria continued to walk down the back streets which fortunately were lit just enough to be able to see smart, elegant houses on each side. The rain continued to pour down and the two women quickened their pace.

'We don't have go through with this, I understand if you're having doubts,' Emily said kindly. 'After all you've been through, it's understandable to have some reservations and even feel a little scared.'

Victoria hesitated. 'We've come this far, I think we should at least make it to the house.'

Emily looked at her friend who like herself was drenched. Victoria's glasses had steamed up and she took them off in an effort to dry them. It would be easy to turn back and walk away despite all the efforts made to come tonight.

Emily once again was reminded of Victoria's sadness, a sadness that had become a heavy burden which she carried. Victoria needed to know the truth and Emily hoped she could be rewarded tonight by answers from the past and perhaps closure would be given.

'It can't be much further, let me look again at the address,' Victoria said as she rummaged through her bag.

With cold hands, she held up a crumpled piece of paper which she unfolded trying in vain not to get it wet. She read the address again, 26 Humphries Row. The weather was closing in and they needed to get away from the streets and into the warmth. Emily noticed the street sign hung precariously marking the end of the road.

'This is Humphries Street so Humphries Row must be nearby.'

'Yes, it's got to be near,' agreed Victoria.

The wind continuously howled along the street making Victoria shiver. Emily wanted to let her friend know that she could turn back and go home if she wanted.

'Look Vicky, I realise tonight means a lot to you.'

'Yes, it does.'

'It may however, not be as easy as you think,' Emily reasoned. 'I just don't want you to be disappointed in what you may find out.'

The death of her Victoria's fiancé had come as a cruel blow. Victoria had never recovered from her tragic loss and Emily suspected she never would.

As they turned the corner, the street sign confirmed they were now on Humphries Row. Looking at the numbers of each house, 26 was at the far end of the row of terraces.

Each house was identical to the next. Tall windows with shutters and green wooden doors greeted them boasting panes of glass allowing people to peep inside to see just enough without seeing too much. Emily knocked on the door several times but each time there was no reply. On the sixth time eventually the door opened. An odd looking woman stepped forwards.

'Good evening ladies, I believe you must be Victoria and Emily,' the woman said beckoning for them to enter. 'You'd better come in. I'm Lily Smith' she said as she held out her hand to greet them.

'Thank you,' Emily stepped forward feeling the braver of the two.

Lily looked to be older than Emily imagined perhaps in her late forties. Her greying hair was worn scraped neatly back in a bun which served to emphasise her thin face. Lily's eyes were piercing blue. Her skin was so white, it glowed in the darkness of the hallway of the house.

Lily was in fact the reason Emily and Victoria had come to Humphries Row and had made their way through London's busy streets on such a foul night.

Lily had been recommended by Joyce, a close friend from the firm of solicitors where Victoria had worked several years ago. Lily's services however were of no ordinary matter. Lily was in fact a clairvoyant, a psychic, a medium, a woman who some say spoke to the spirits beyond our world.

It was the war that had made Lily busy in her line of work. War and its tragic losses and more importantly, the loss of loved ones. That of course is what had happened to Victoria and that is why she was here tonight.

The man she had loved and lost and had so wanted to marry had been a casualty of war. Before Harry's death, Emily knew her friend would have never even contemplated visiting a woman of the occult but Emily now understood that death can do that to people, it brings them crashing to their knees until what was once the unthinkable becomes real.

Emily was unsure whether she believed in spirits and that it was possible to contact them from beyond the grave but she wanted to help her friend and that was reason enough for her being here tonight. The part of her that did believe in ghosts, felt apprehensive as they entered. She sensed a cold, eerie presence which strengthened as she went further inside. A strange musty smell hung heavy in the air.

'This way,' Lily said as she quickly ushered them to the back of the house.

They soon entered one of the larger rooms which ran parallel to what looked to be a long thin garden. Emily politely acknowledged the people sitting round the table and Victoria nodded her head looking more uneasy by the minute and glancing at her friend for some reassurance. The room fell silent apart from the clock on the sideboard which made a loud ticking noise.

Lily stood at the head of the table addressing its occupants which were mainly made up of women though two men sat at the end, perhaps like Victoria they too had lost partners.

Lily was only a small woman but her presence soon filled the room and although she was softly spoken, her voice quickly became louder.

'Hold hands everyone, for tonight we contact love ones of the past,' she said.

Ten pairs of hands nervously joined together to form a circle along the panels of the table. Emily glanced at Victoria who looked terrified. Emily knew her friend well enough to sense that she seemed to be having doubts about the evening. Minutes passed but the room remained still. Then suddenly a loud scream could be heard. Emily thought it had come from outside the room and she tightened her grip of Victoria.

A second scream followed louder than the first. Then there was silence. Emily's heart was beating fast, she wanted to get up but her body seemed unable to move. She stared transfixed at the table, as though in a trance.

The cloth on the table moved and a cold breeze blew across the floor. The curtains started to sway and footsteps sounded slowly as if being dragged across the floorboards. Emily noticed that Lily looked disturbed. Perhaps this presence was more than she'd anticipated.

'Speak to us, send us your message,' Lily said her voice remaining calm. No sooner as she had said this, a wall lamp fell to the floor. Splinters of glass shattered loudly crashing on the floor.

'Do not break the circle, whatever happens, you must not break the circle for the spirit is near, I sense it's a woman and she is now with us in this room, come to us, show yourself,' Lily beckoned.

Emily clenched her hands through fear and the rest of the group remained completely still. A groaning sound could now be heard and once more the curtains swung from side to side. Lily had to shout to be heard over the noise which seemed unbearable.

'Speak your piece and be gone, go now and take all what is with you away, far way,' commanded Lily.

Then as if by some gigantic force of nature, Emily's chair was swept from beneath her feet. To her horror she found herself being pulled by a force that was so strong it took her breath away.

'Stop this, stop it at once,' Emily screamed trying to hold on to some furniture as she was dragged to the door which swung open. 'I beg you to stop.'

Instinctively Emily knew she was being pushed to the top of the flight of stairs. She tried desperately to grab something, anything as her body was pulled but it was useless, she couldn't stop it. The circle was now broken and people were frantically scrambling to their feet trying to help but it was too late.

They all heard the crashing sound as Emily was forced down the stairs.

When she woke the next morning, Emily was aware that she was in a strange bed and as she put her hand to sooth her throbbing head, she felt a bandage that had been strapped across her forehead and tied at the nape of her neck.

'Ha, you're awake, thank goodness, lucky I'd say, damned lucky, by all accounts the fall was stopped by some boxes that had been left at the foot of the stairs,' Victoria said sympathetically. 'I think somebody was looking out for you after all.'

'Where am I?' Emily asked still coming to terms with last night's strange encounter. 'My head hurts so much.'

'James, bless him, wanted you in hospital but instead I've brought you back to my parents' house. James will be back soon, he wanted to get you some fresh flowers, he's such a dear.'

'What happened last night Vicky?' Emily asked her head still throbbing.

'Well, it seems that your favour for me darling backfired somewhat. We didn't contact Harry... the thing is Emily whatever was in that room last night, it came for you. Whoever do you think it was?' Victoria asked her friend. 'It was a frightening experience, that's for sure.'

Victoria felt sad that she didn't contact her fiancé but right now her thoughts were for Emily and that concerned her far more although she couldn't explain why she felt that way, perhaps she felt guilty, after all she'd been desperate to attend the seance and because of that Emily had been hurt. The occult was something that was frowned upon and Victoria was a strict Catholic but she had wanted answers.

She looked closely at her friend, they had known each other since Emily had moved to London some years before. Victoria suddenly had a feeling that there was a side to her friend that she didn't quite know and perhaps never would. Some things in life are better left unspoken and Victoria felt that this was one.

'I don't understand what happened,' Emily said at last but looked distracted as she spoke.

'Well, I don't think I will be doing a seance again and I bet you feel exactly the same.'

'No, I don't think I will,' Emily said and smiled.

Victoria was a good friend and she didn't want to upset her. Emily's body ached from head to toe but at least she felt safe in Victoria's family home. James would take her back home in a few days and she would then have time to rest. Her eyes felt heavy and started to close but she struggled to keep awake.

Victoria wanting her friend to sleep, quietly closed the door shut. As Emily drifted in and out of sleep, she couldn't stop thinking about the events of last night, it had frightened her more than she wanted to admit. Being dragged across the floor had been a terrifying experience.

Emily pulled the bed covers around her. She knew exactly who had been trying to scare her and why but she didn't want to tell Victoria, it was a part of her past she needed to forget. She regretted the seance, she'd been caught off guard, she would need to be more careful. She'd been lucky until now but Emily was wise enough to know that sooner or later luck runs out. With such disturbed thoughts she reluctantly fell into a troubled night's sleep.


Two years later

As the train pulled away from Kings Cross Station, Emily fastened her coat conscious of the cold winter's night and the ten hour ride through to Hull. It was a long journey ahead and Emily knew it would mean a late arrival so sensibly she had chosen to spend the night in Hull and the following morning, catch the connecting train up the north east line.

She felt tired from her early morning start and welcomed the train not being too busy. Not many passengers had embarked in London and Emily was pleased to find she had a carriage to herself.

The train was about to set off, when a lady wearing a nurses' uniform suddenly got on.

'Oh, thank goodness I managed to get this train,' the woman said. 'I'm Sophie by the way. I'm afraid I've got the long ride all the way up to Hull.'

'Emily and very pleased to meet you,' Emily held out her hand to Sophie. 'Please take the seat next to me,' Emily said kindly and moved her bag to let Sophie sit. 'I'm hoping we manage to have the carriage to ourselves.'

'Well, it looks like a good day to travel, are you sure you don't mind sharing your carriage, after all we have a long journey together?' Sophie asked politely.

'Not at all, I'll be glad of the company,' Emily said. 'Are you local to London?'

Emily put her glasses down and the book she had been reading.

Sophie looked red faced, shifting uncomfortably in her seat. 'I'm living in Pinner at the moment but I've lived all over London.'

Sophie's awkwardness surprised Emily. It was as though she didn't really want to talk about herself. Emily looked carefully at her new travelling companion. Sophie's hair was scraped off her face in a neat bun which was held by a slide. She had a pretty face with brown eyes and although she smiled often, Emily couldn't help notice a sadness etched in her face. Her nurses uniform seemed to be ill fitting and far too big for her tiny frame, it almost gave the impression of not belonging to her.

Minutes later the train chugged its way down the lines of Kings Cross Station leading to the north of the country. London started to fade into the distance and so began a lovely peaceful journey with small villages and towns coming into view and disappearing just as quickly.

'Do you often travel to Hull?' Sophie asked politely.

'Years ago I did but not so much these days,' Emily said. 'I'm actually traveling to see my friend who lives nearby. She was a house keeper at one of the Halls just up the coast,' Emily said as she shuffled in her seat trying to get comfortable. 'Of course, it was a long time ago. Even to this day she tells the most wonderful stories from her time there. Herron Hall is a very grand house in the north of the country.'

'Outside Hull is it?' Sophie asked. 'Only, when I was a young girl, I spent some time around there.'

'Yes, it's just outside the seaside town of Whitby,' Emily answered.

'So where does your friend live now?' Sophie asked.

'Still near Whitby though it's slightly in land, a small village called Helmsley, pretty place it is.'

Sophie listened but seemed oddly distracted. As Emily watched Sophie, a strange thought crossed her mind, she had that knowing feeling that somehow she recognised Sophie. Maybe she reminded her of somebody that she had known in her past. But as hard as she thought, for the life of her she couldn't remember where from.

It had been warm on the train and Emily welcomed the cool breeze that blew in from the open windows. The sun was beginning to lose its intense heat making it more pleasant for travelling.

'I've heard of Herron Hall,' Sophie remarked suddenly wanting to go back to the story. 'In fact, people say the Hall is haunted. Wasn't there some terrible murders that took place years ago?'

Emily hesitated before answering. Although she'd mentioned the Hall in passing, she hadn't planned on talking about Herron Hall. She allowed herself to pause.

'That's right, the murders took place just before my friend Susan started working there.'

Sophie nodded which seemed to be a signal for Emily to continue.

'As I said it was a long time ago and stories as you know get changed over the years,' Emily said.

'Yes of course, but your friend, she must have quite a story to tell from her time at the Hall?'

'Well yes...' Emily said who was feeling a bit tired but continued. 'Susan was actually brought up on the Herron Estate as a young girl, her parents worked there and her grandparents before that.

The house was sold soon after the murders and Susan stayed at the Hall and worked for the family who moved up from London. Sadly they only lived there for a few years, understandably it was a very difficult place to live in.'

'What happened to the Hall after that?' Sophie asked straightening her uniform which looked crumpled from sitting.

'After that I believe that the Hall was bought and sold several more times in quick succession until at last the present family decided to stay,' Emily explained.

'The Hall must have been very affected?'

'Yes, I believe it was,' Emily said.

Again Emily looked at Sophie who looked so familiar. Emily was tired but as everybody knows, once you start a story it's very difficult to stop.

'So did Susan work for the Fischer family who lived at the Hall after the Green family moved from there?' Sophie asked.

So far in the conversation Emily hadn't mentioned the Fischer's name and was surprised of Sophie's knowledge of the story. As Emily sat there, surprise turned to suspicion and again she felt a strange unease as she looked at Sophie which made her feel wary.

Emily felt Sophie knew more about the murders of Herron Hall than she was letting on. Secrets of the past, always have a way of sneaking up on you especially when you're not expecting them. Emily felt her throat tighten and an uncomfortable atmosphere filled the carriage. Emily didn't want Sophie to know about her nagging doubts so she carried on talking, perhaps she thought, if she told the story she could judge Sophie's reaction as to what her motives were. Yes, that's what she'd do, she'd tell the story.

People's faces have a tendency to talk in a silent language all of their own and after all what more could she do she reasoned.

'Yes,' Emily went on. 'Susan worked at the Hall. She was a hard worker and not surprisingly before long she became Head Housekeeper,' Emily explained. 'You see as time passed it was a role that would not suit all.'

'Really.'

'Susan was happy for the first year,' Emily explained. 'Mrs. Fischer instantly fell in love with the Hall though her husband was never as keen.'

'Can you describe the family?' Sophie asked.

'Mr. Fischer was a wealthy man and in his spare time,' Emily continued. 'He worked as a botanist at Kew Gardens. He worked abroad for most of the year and so it was Mrs. Fischer who Susan spent most of her time.

Hannah Fischer was a kind gentle woman with a nervous disposition and the lonely nights spent without her husband meant that she befriended Susan. The role of Head Housekeeper should have been perfect however after a couple of months Susan was soon reminded of the Hall's troubled past.'

'What happened exactly?' Sophie asked.

'Well...a part of Susan's job meant she often had to visit the kitchens late at night. It was lonely down in the basements of the Hall and Susan didn't enjoy being there on her own. Mrs. Fischer often commented that the house had a certain presence but Susan had taken this to be none other than idle chat. The Hall itself was part of a little village and people as you know tend to gossip and exaggerate stories.'

'Yes,' Sophie agreed. 'But I can imagine some old houses can be cold.'

'Maybe,' Emily nodded. 'However one evening just as night came, Susan felt a terrible sense of dread. The Hall is rather exposed and susceptible to bad weather especially being so high up on the moors. That night there was a strong wind which blew from outside making strange noises around the room.

Susan tried to busy herself but the wind held strong making the windows rattle. As Susan was about to leave the kitchen, she saw a strange sight, it was of a woman who stood before her. She began to panic, Susan looked around and became even more frightened when she knew there was only one way into the kitchens. The door had remained closed all evening and nobody could have got passed without her noticing. The room became extremely cold and an eeriness filled the kitchens.

'Was the woman a ghost, is that what you're saying?'

'Perhaps she was, that we'll never know,' Emily said. 'When Susan told me the story, she was sure she had seen a ghost. She described a scar on the woman's face which ran down her cheek. She wore a white dress with lace perhaps suggesting she may have lived in the house not as a servant but as part of the family.'

'Susan must have been terrified?' Sophie said quietly, shocked by the story. 'I can't even imagine how she must have felt being there on her own.'

'She was,' Emily explained. 'The fact that she stood alone made her more frightened.'

'Did she leave her position?' Sophie asked.

'No.' Emily replied. 'But she knew her days at the Hall were coming to an end, for no matter how kind Mrs. Fischer was, Susan could not have any more of those scares.'

'Did she?'

'Unfortunately yes, I'm afraid those chilling apparitions carried on, Susan saw objects being thrown around and often could hear terrible wailing sounds in the corridors. She started to dread being there on her own especially if she had to work evenings,' Emily explained.

'But why didn't Susan leave?' Sophie asked.

'Well naturally it would have been the most sensible thing to do but Mrs. Fischer needed Susan more than ever,' Emily explained. 'They both hoped that a calm would come over the Hall and the hauntings would eventually stop but alas it was not to be, for each week that passed there appeared more sightings and disturbances. After a few months the presence at the Hall became so unbearable that a local priest was asked to exorcise the building.'

'Did it work?' Susan asked.

'No I'm afraid not,' Emily answered. 'Sadly, no. But it seemed his efforts were not in vain after all. What did come about was why the Hall was haunted in the first place. The priest had known the Green family and was able to confirm that he believed the spirit to be that of Bella Green. It was her troubled spirit that was the cause of the ghostly happenings. Perhaps…' Emily looked at her companion who seemed to be keenly listening. 'Perhaps like I'm telling you now, it was a time that Father Simmonds needed to unburden himself of the sorry tale. It therefore came about that one evening along with Mrs. Fischer and Susan, he sat down by an open fire in a neighbouring Inn and decided to share the secrets of Bella Green and the downfall of Herron Hall.'

'So, you know the tale itself?' Sophie's voice broke through Emily's thoughts. 'It's just for a second or two, you looked like you were far back in the past.'

'Yes, I know the tale of the Hall and you're right about going back in the past especially as you get to my age, the past is always with you in some way,' Emily said thoughtfully.

'So, what did Father Simmonds tell Susan?' Sophie asked her eyes darting excitedly.

'It's a long story and so it's rather fortunate that we have a very long journey ahead of us.'

Emily sighed and glanced back to the window ready to recount her tale.

Emily was a quiet woman who generally kept about her own business, yet here was a chance to unburden a tale that had troubled her for too long.

It was as if by chance, perhaps a meeting of fate had brought the two women together that evening. And so as the train passed through fields in a never ending landscape, the story of Herron Hall was told and maybe for one of the last times.

# Chapter 2

The North Yorkshire coast is notorious for being rugged with a wild beauty which even on the greyest of days is bewitching. For most of the year, grey clouds from the North Sea cover the sky which eventually give way to summer. As the summer months fade however and winter sets, sea fogs frequent the shore lines.

Those fogs act as a blanket that shroud the coast making it have an eeriness that envelops the quaint seaside villages and not surprisingly tales of ghosts and strange occurrences have been recounted for generations.

The story of Bella Green has remained almost a secret but perhaps is one of the most sinister and chilling tales of them all. It is believed even to this day, villagers still talk about the hauntings of her ghost both in and around Herron Hall. Bella's troubled spirit is still the cause of strange unearthly happenings and noises that come from the house particularly in the winter months as the nights draw in and daylight is lost.

By all accounts, Herron Hall was once a happy place until a series of events led to a dreadful cruel night where lives were lost in the most tragic of circumstances. Herron Hall is the grandest of houses, set in over three hundred acres of land mainly used for agriculture. At the time, valuable collections of art works hung from the many walls and other priceless antiques could be seen in the vast corridors and rooms. It truly was a spectacular house and even to this day remains so.

Bella was born of noble aristocracy. She married David Green, a rich American businessman whose own father George, had captained a large merchant ship sailing round the world. It would be fair to say that he knew the waters of the West Indies like the back of his hand. The trade winds it seems had served him well and soon he became a very wealthy man. His real fortune however came from the world of banking and sadly this proved to be his last venture before his death. His wealth however ensured that both his sons, David and Edward were left with a vast fortune upon his death.

David was a charming man and not only had he inherited his father's fortunes, he also had his charismatic manner. He was naturally generous in nature and his easy going charms made him successful in business.

Bella on the other hand had a quiet nature and a discordant manner and unlike her husband remained unpopular at the Hall.

David and Bella led an extravagant lifestyle and held lavish parties which were ranked highly even in London circles. It seemed however that almost from the start of their marriage Bella was difficult to live with and David was disappointed by his wife's selfish behaviour.

When at last Bella fell pregnant, David felt sure this would change things between them but alas Bella only became more withdrawn. David was of course delighted but to his immense disappointment his much wanted and longed for son was not to be, instead only Mary was born.

Mary was very much like her father, independent with a fierce determination, perfect to manage her father's business. Mary however was no fool and knew as a woman, this could never be. Mary lived a privileged life and was very confident. She mixed easily with her parent's friends yet felt just as happy to be with the staff of the Hall. Being able to circumnavigate with all echelons of society is a true gift, one that Mary was born with.

Pretty, with brown eyes and wavy blond hair, Mary had stunning looks, she was a real beauty. Bella knew her daughter's looks could be traded for a very wealthy husband. In truth David didn't give a fig who Mary married so long as she was happy but he knew his wife had different plans. She wanted her daughter to marry for power and wealth, with little consideration for love or friendship.

Growing up Mary was aware that she would not be able to marry of choice. The head housekeeper, George's son was never going to figure in her mother's plans. She was close to Jimmy, although five years older, he had always been very kind to her and they had been friends for many years.

It was only when she was seventeen and Jimmy twenty two that she realised how fond of him she was. He had been training in London to be a police officer and one weekend, he made an unexpected visit.

When he entered the room that evening, Mary knew that no other man would ever make her feel the way he did. Mary didn't see him as young Jimmy anymore but instead a very striking man. A man she realised she had always loved and would be forever in love with. She knew in Jimmy he would love her back and always take care of her.

She tried to tell herself it was no more than infatuation, he was older and very handsome but she knew he liked her but perhaps for now no more than a friend. And so it was that as he went away that weekend, any hope of anything more than friendship faded.

She knew it could never be as her mother had quickly made the situation very clear, that although Jimmy was a very nice young man he wasn't however the type of man Mary would marry. As Mary listened to her mother's protests, she knew that if Jimmy couldn't have her heart then no other man would ever have it too. From time to time, Jimmy would visit the Hall and Mary could only look from afar, aware that by each visit, he would look even more dashing than before. His dark hair and green eyes almost melting her inside.

Mary knew the truth, Jimmy was out of reach, someone she would never have. By the time she was nineteen, her mother was keen to marry her off to someone rich and by then Jimmy had found Ida. In Mary's mind Jimmy was even more removed, only now in her imagination.

Her father therefore had little choice other than to find a husband for his daughter. Marriage would be traded for wealth and that's all there was to it, love it seemed would play no part. Despite Bella's ambitions for her daughter, David knew how important it was to choose a suitable man for Mary. If he were to choose the wrong man then there would be no going back. Once the deal was done it was unbreakable.

The enormous task in hand had caused him countless nights of unrest but he had assured himself that Mary was after all in an enviable position. She was not only beautiful but also had great wealth. David had no doubt before the coming Christmas she would be engaged with a summer wedding to follow.

It was therefore decided that a Ball would be held at the Hall and this hopefully would be the opportunity for Mary to meet her future husband.

Several eligible young men were to be invited that met a strict criteria.

One evening David was summoned by his wife to compile a list of wealthy young eligible bachelors. He didn't have to think long, his wife had already thought for him.

# Chapter 3

The train pulled into a small station, allowing Emily to pause the story. Some of the passengers collected their luggage from the above racks and were busy looking for their connecting trains. The sun was beginning to sink into the sky leaving trails of red on the horizon, daylight was fading and dusk was nearing.

'So, this Mary Green what happened at the Ball, the house would have looked wonderful?' Sophie asked. 'Was this the night that Mary met her husband or did Jimmy save her?'

'Ah, the Ball, let me think, yes that evening changed everything,' Emily said. 'You're correct, Herron Hall looked magnificent even though the frosts had visited early that winter. The main building with its many tall windows had been carefully lit for the evening.'

'What about Mary was she excited?' Sophie asked. 'It's just that you haven't mentioned her much in the story, tell me about her?'

'No, perhaps I haven't,' Emily replied. 'I think Mary was oblivious to all the preparations, she led a privileged life and such evenings it was fair to say were quite common. What I can say is that Mary was adamant she didn't want a husband but she was sensible and knew sooner or later she would have no choice other than to marry.'

'What did she wear for such an occasion?' Sophie asked keen to know as though building a picture of the evening in her mind.

'By all accounts, I believe Mary looked perfect very much like her mother who was also very beautiful. She was only small with a slender delicate frame but somehow her presence like her father could fill a room.

Mary admired herself in the mirror. She fitted perfectly into a silk dress which had been sourced from a boutique not far from Green Park. Her chosen outfit with its narrow waist along with a pearl necklace and matching earrings made her look even more beautiful. Mary entered the ballroom as planned by the main stairs. She wanted all eyes to be on her and naturally she achieved the desired effect.

That evening her father had three particular suiters in mind, Charles Denson being the first. A young respectable gentleman from the North East. His family's business originated from mining stock, from the humblest of beginnings, delivering coal door to door for local villagers. Charles now worked for his father. The luck of black coal it would seem had covered the family in riches, wealth which would last for many years to come.

The second young man, Henry Dawson was a graduate from Oxford, who'd then gone onto study law at Harvard and had since worked in London.

His aristocratic background made him a favourite choice. His family throughout generations owned by all accounts quite a few streets around Kensington Gardens. His family lived in Hampshire in Gosforth Hall and bred race horses just as a hobby.

Lastly, there was Albert Smithers whose father frequently did business with David Green. Most of their wealth was invested in farmland and ranches in mid America. It was said that the last few years of harvesting, had provided them with a small fortune.

Albert Smithers alongside his father James could often be seen in London's Gentleman's Clubs in and around the city. Albert was a good looking man, a man who knew he was good looking which made him flawed with an arrogant nature. He was however probably the most likely of the three that would suit Mary but David was aware of his reputedly roving eye for the ladies. He hoped for stability for Mary but perhaps this wasn't what Albert wanted.

The word player suited Albert and his dark smouldering looks certainly did nothing only to enhance his charm and charisma. He was undoubtedly a dashing beau. As Mary came down those stairs that night at Herron Hall; her fate was inevitably sealed.

Henry and Charles, could only stand by and watch as Mary seemed smitten by the dashing Albert Smithers. Both men soon realised this and quickly turned their attentions to the other ladies amongst the guests.

'Well, well, your father never mentioned to me that he had such a stunning daughter,' Albert said whilst taking Mary's hand.

'Thank you,' Mary said smiling politely.

'I can't think it was an oversight on your father's behalf but perhaps he wisely wanted to hide you away from bad men like me.'

Albert laughed. He was confident Mary could see that. For all her airs of sophistication she knew she was no match for this degree of showmanship and because she had drank a little too much wine she started to feel giddy and light headed.

'Well,' she retorted unsure of what to say next. 'My father also must have forgotten to mention the mysterious Albert Smithers.'

Mary allowed Albert to kiss her hand.

'Well it seems we are both in luck, Mary Green, though its cold outside, shall we avoid such formalities and escape to your summer house in the garden?' Albert said.

Mary couldn't help but smile, here was a man who wouldn't take no for an answer. Albert slipped his arm in hers and she found herself being led outside. Mary felt apprehensive. Albert seemed determined to win her over. She knew her mother would approve of him. He fitted her choice exactly she could see that. The problem was he didn't fit hers. Mary's mother could be forceful. She would have to share her concerns with her father but for now she would have to pretend to play her part, that of a dutiful daughter.

'I'm sorry I was a little forward just now but I tend not to feel at home on such formal occasions,' Albert said whilst loosening his tie. 'I hate having to wear these damned things,' he said and laughed.

Albert gently slipped his arm through Mary's. 'Anyway, let's have that walk now, the night is still young after all.'

'Why not,' Mary said glad at last to get some fresh air.

Mary thought Albert's manner much too forward causing her to feel hesitant. Out of politeness she found herself being led by a man who felt very much like a stranger, a stranger she knew she would never really know nor did she want to. Mary was clever enough to hide her reservations, she had been brought up to be polite, it was expected of her.

'Of course, we can go out by the side doors, the orangery is not too far,' she said trying to sound calm.

Mary pointed in the direction of the walled garden. The cold air worked well and thankfully brought Mary to her senses. Away from the Hall, Albert looked different. His good looks and chiselled face made him seem almost charming. Mary admitted to herself that it would be quite easy to be swept away by him in some romantic tryst however she was now in the business to find a suitable husband and looks and charm weren't even considered. That dream was over. Jimmy was just a thing of the past. The thought of him made her feel sad. Jimmy was twice the man Albert was or could ever be.

'Our fathers would like us to be more than friends,' Albert said and looked at Mary to see her reaction.

'There's a lot of things our fathers would like,' said Mary her voice sounding happier than she was.

'My father generally gets what he wants,' Albert retorted who so far had been surprised by Mary, she seemed far smarter than he had thought.

The orangery of Herron Hall was beautifully decorated. Gold edging trimmed the doors and carefully placed garden lights flickered against the clear winter sky. Albert bent his head toward Mary and suddenly kissed her.

Mary was surprised, she hadn't expected this forwardness and it certainly wasn't befitting of a gentleman but from the second she had met Albert, she realised he wasn't one. In an odd way, the kiss had felt nice, only because as she closed her eyes she had only thought of Jimmy. Mary had to remain strong. She felt in a terrible dilemma, she knew she needed a husband and here was a man who fitted her mother's list, rich, socially connected and had business interests in the right places.

Mary sighed, how she wished her life was simple and she could marry someone she loved. She couldn't even allow herself to think of Jimmy.

She felt trapped and knew that Albert was not the man to save her.

'That was a special kiss just as tonight has been,' Albert said.

'Yes, it has,' Mary replied politely.

She felt numb and tried to sound more plausible for her mother's sake making sure she returned a smile. 'Maybe our fathers are right after all but we won't tell them that,' Mary remarked and laughed more from nerves.

'I have a feeling that our fathers may soon be very pleased,' Albert said looking at Mary. 'I really like you Mary.'

Mary bit her lip and considered what to say next, she felt it was best to keep Albert dangling. For now she would play along with this charade and buy herself some time, which seemed important. What was it her father always taught her, wriggle room, yes that was it, wriggle room.

Mary was all too aware that there was a great deal of pressure for her to marry but not just with anybody but with a man who had the necessary means to keep her in the life she was accustomed to.

Mary was trying to think practically. Albert Smithers was making all the advances towards her. She was considering her options so why she thought to herself, should she foolishly show her hand now. Albert was by no means ideal but he may prove to be a good husband after all.

'I think my guests will be wondering where I am,' Mary said glad to break the awkward silence. 'Shall we go back to the Ball?'

As they walked back inside, it gave Mary a chance to think what it would be like to be engaged and then married. Wisdom told her that society was a far better place for a married woman, it meant being accepted and respected, things that were important for someone in her position.

As the evening drew to a close, not surprisingly there was a general feeling amongst the guests that Mary had already made her choice of partner, a fact that by no means wasn't wasted on her own mother. Mary winced as she knew her mother's eagerness and determination would now act as a catalyst for marriage. As the guests were leaving Albert went over to Mary.

He spoke softly into Mary's ear. 'My parents would very much like to invite you to our family home in Sussex?' Albert asked and coughed nervously which surprised Mary. 'My mother is already making preparations for the weekend. Please do say yes, I think you will really enjoy your visit,' Albert said almost in a desperate tone.

Mary smiled to herself and couldn't resist to appear nonchalant, she was actually enjoying teasing Albert. It felt nice to have the upper hand though she feared once married this would be short lived.

'I can't say at the moment Albert as I have my father's business to think of and there's of course the holiday period which is fast approaching,' Mary said. 'Christmas is a very busy time for us.' She sensed immediately it was the right thing to say buying her some time.

'Very well, but I will be devastated if you don't agree,' Albert said trying not to sound too disappointed. 'I hope you find the time Mary as I really want you to be there.'

Mary was a practical girl and was more than aware that marriage in worlds like hers and Albert's was an extension of a business. She knew her parents had wanted a son and perhaps her father saw in Albert someone who could manage his estates. She knew that a bad marriage would be a problem for her parents and if she chose wrongly there would be repercussions for generations to come. '

'I'll of course let you know as soon as I am able.'

It was the best Mary could say. Seeing the disappointment on Albert's face, she quickly added. 'I will try my best.'

After all she didn't want to appear too cold, a man like Albert Smithers would soon lose interest if the game was over before it had begun, so she answered carefully. 'Now I come to think of it, I happen to have a little time in a few weeks just before Christmas. I'm sure it would be a lovely time to visit your home which is not too far from London. ' She paused thinking how pleased Albert looked. 'I've not been to the city for a long time, I love London with its many shops and beautiful parks.'

Mary moved her hair to the side revealing a little coy smile which wasn't wasted on Albert.

'I will look forward to it Mary, don't leave it too long, I would love to spend some time with you.'

'Likewise, and I know that you will make it special,' Mary replied feeling anxious. Albert Smithers she knew would be a man who acted far too quickly, too quickly for a girl like herself.

Already events were taking on a turn of their own and she felt powerless like a pawn in a game of chess that she knew she couldn't win. Mary needed some time to think and by stalling, she would carefully consider the matter in hand.

In fairness there were big orders at the factory and she desperately wanted to help her father. Most of the workforce in the factories were looking to down tools for Christmas. Lately, her father had started to ask her for more help and she didn't want to let him down.

Mary went to bed that evening in a reflective mood weighing up her options. She knew that her days as a single woman would sooner rather than later be over and that thought frightened her. Her parents would insist she were married and fairly soon and she thought that Albert was probably as good as she was going to get. Her dreams of being with Jimmy were fading and a stark reality beckoned, a marriage arranged is what girls like herself were born into. On the surface she had so much but in reality so little.

Albert was far from perfect but he too needed a wife. So as Mary lay in her bed that night, she knew she probably had a husband waiting for her and should feel pleased. Mary however was wise enough to know that once you get what you want in life sometimes it doesn't seem that appealing.

# Chapter 4

Whichever part of the world you're from, Christmas is always a magical time. Winter had set in early around the north east coast and the keen frosts of November had brought about the first flurries of snow. By the time December had arrived a white coating covered most of the surrounding hills.

Herron Hall is situated quite high on those moors and for a few days the house had been inaccessible to the outside world.

This had not suited Mary's plans at all, now bored and restless she reconsidered Albert Smithers' invitation to stay at his home, Sewter Lodge which along with the poor weather now seemed far more appealing. She had always liked London, with its busy streets, bright lights and glamorous shops. Albert's home wasn't a far ride away which made it perfect for a few visits to the theatres and such like.

As much as she hated to admit it, a change of scenery would be a good thing. She also thought it would be an opportunity to get to know Albert better. She needed to see what he was really like, Also if she didn't like him, she knew her father wouldn't agree to the marriage. He loved his daughter and deep down Mary knew he only wanted her to be happy. Mary therefore wrote a polite but short letter to Albert explaining that she would like to accept his generous hospitality.

It was a good day's ride by car down to Sussex and it was agreed that Mary's chauffeur would act as a chaperone throughout her trip.

George was a trusted member of staff as well as a personal friend to David. He was also Jimmy's father. George and Charlotte had worked for Mary's family for the best part of fifteen years, Mary was very fond of them. To her they were family and had always been so kind to her.

As she thought of George, her mind was immediately diverted to Jimmy. It reminded her of how much she was still in love with him but also how hopeless the situation was. She'd heard that he'd recently been promoted and by all accounts had been made an Inspector. No matter how impressed Mary was of Jimmy's promotion it sadly was wasted on her mother. To be Mary's choice of partner was simply out of the question. It was a terrible sadness that Mary carried with her. Albert could only be a poor substitute.

As Mary got in the car, she noticed George seemed nervous and wondered why, he surely wasn't aware of her feelings towards his son.

'Is everything alright George?' Mary asked politely.

'Yes Mary, I'm sorry, I was just wrapped in my own thoughts that's all. Thankfully it's a wonderful day to be travelling as it appears at last to be a little warmer,' George replied trying hard to make polite conversation.

'Yes, that biting wind seems for now to have stopped and besides it's always a little warmer in the south,' Mary said. 'Though I know we have a long journey ahead of us.'

'Yes but fortunately, I have good company for such a journey,' laughed George.

George was a kind man much like his son Jimmy. Mary was grateful he was going to be accompanying her. His wife Charlotte also worked on the estate. Her father rather generously had given them a lodge by the river. They had been over the moon at the time but David had made it clear that it was the least he could do for all their hard work.

As she sat in the car, she thought of Jimmy. Although they were from very different backgrounds, they had always been good friends. Mary had often played with him as a little girl and as they had got older, they would ride together. Like herself, Jimmy had a keen interest in horses. Mary always made a point to ask George or Charlotte how Jimmy was getting along. His life seemed so exciting and mysterious. She knew she could never feel the same about Albert as she would Jimmy. Mary sadly knew Jimmy was always something she couldn't have.

Throughout most of the journey, George and Mary chatted away mostly about Jimmy. Although the conversation flowed along, Mary couldn't help but notice that George didn't seem himself and wondered if it had anything to do with Albert.

'Are you sure you're alright, it's just you seem very quiet George?' Mary asked knowing full well that something was bothering him.

'Yes, Mary, I just want you to be careful that's all, sometimes you have your mother's impetuous nature.'

This surprised Mary as she had never thought of her mother as having an impetuous manner in fact her mother seemed far too cold in nature to be impetuous. George bit his lip as he said it and Mary instinctively knew that he now regretted his comment.

'I'm glad you're accompanying me,' Mary said. 'I feel quite nervous and unsure what to expect.'

'Just watch your back,' George said. 'I'm afraid you're quite trusting and perhaps a tad naive Mary.'

'Yes, I am. But I will be careful and I know you're there with me.'

Mary felt anxious by George's comments and decided she didn't want to pursue the matter. She thought it best to say no more. She was also surprised knowing perhaps there was a side to her mother that she didn't quite know.

As they approached the house, Mary could see that Sewter Lodge was no less grand than Mary's own home. The approach to the Lodge was elegant and the vast gardens at the front of the house had been cultivated with small neat hedges and ornate statues that lined the drive on both sides. Albert stood waiting at the main entrance to the house. He politely embraced her and took her luggage which seemed a nice gesture to Mary. Albert had good manners, a quality that Mary appreciated.

'I'm so glad you decided to accept our invitation.'

'So am I, although the journey always seems longer around London than I remember.'

Albert nodded in agreement. 'Naturally, my parents are both excited to have you as their guest,' Albert said taking Mary's hand and leading her inside the Lodge.

'Thank you, it's such a beautiful house and of course made all the more special this time of year,' Mary remarked as she stepped into the main hall.

'Yes, we love Christmas and the house always looks at its best,' Albert added.

'When was it built?' Mary asked politely.

'Around 1790, so it's quite old but my grandfather bless him, made the house twice as big,' Albert explained.

'Well, it looks very special,' Mary said trying to sound enthusiastic.

Inwardly though she felt nervous and still didn't feel comfortable around Albert. It wasn't that he was unfriendly but there was something about his manner that she didn't trust but for now she couldn't quite put her finger as to why she felt that way.

As Mary followed Albert up the main staircase, she was surprised by the decor, here the house did not seem so elegant. Mary couldn't help compare her own home to the Lodge. Herron Hall boasted unusual treasures that had been collected mainly by her grandfather from all around the world. At Sewter Lodge, Mary observed, there were a few collections of paintings which hung in the main drawing room which she admired, apart from this touch of grandeur, the truth was Albert's home seemed almost ordinary.

'And lastly here is your room,' Albert said beckoning towards the last door on the corridor.

Mary walked towards a very elegant room with a dressing area and bed that was almost at odds with the rest of the house.

'This is beautiful,' Mary said aware she wanted to appear polite and grateful for Albert's invitation. 'The wallpaper reminds me when I visited Paris last year, it's very continental.'

'I'm pleased you like the room, I visited Paris a while back, it's a lovely city. Come now we can take a stroll into the front room and you can see our famous Christmas tree which I know you will love.'

Mary realised what a difficult situation she found herself. She didn't want to encourage Albert as she was very undecided about him. Away from the safety of home she felt alone and vulnerable. In Mary's mind this visit was after all only a way to really think about whether she could marry Albert. At the moment she still she thought had a choice.

The main front room of the house was finely decorated and the Christmas tree didn't disappoint, it was spectacular with elegant trimmings. As they were admiring the festivities, Albert talked about his family.

'My mother is from Russia, she lived as a young girl just outside St. Petersburg, which is a beautiful city even now despite all the political turmoil. There everybody loves Christmas especially decorating the tree and that's why the tree looks fantastic.'

'It looks very pretty,' Mary said admiringly. 'She must have spent a long time arranging the decorations.'

'It's my mother's project, I'm afraid I have nothing to do with it, other than to admire such beauty.' Albert said as he turned to look at Mary. 'Just as now I look at you. '

'Thank you,' was all Mary could say.

Mary smiled cautiously wondering if Albert was genuinely telling her the truth or just reciting a well used line in his repertoire.

'Well I hope that you are listening because I do mean it and I just want you to know,' Albert said and then paused for a while as if wondering whether or not to ask the next question. 'Have you ever been in love Mary?'

'Yes,' Mary replied honestly thinking of Jimmy. 'Have you Albert?'

'Yes, I have but it was a long time ago,' Albert said as though wanting to tell her more but managing to stop himself before from doing so.

Mary realised that he too was under pressure from his parents and that was a fact they both had in common. They were alike in the fact that marriage was a business. Mary was aware that her father seemed to approve of Albert and that meant a lot to her. Mary was only young but her parents wanted her to settle down as she would then be married.

'My parents would really like us to dine with them this evening, in fact so much so that they have taken the liberty of inviting some family friends, the Edmunds and Bickerstaffs, I don't know if you're acquainted?'

Mary shook her head. 'No, I can't think I know of them.'

'So, it potentially could be rather a full house,' Albert said hoping that Mary had packed clothes for such an occasion.

'Don't worry, I have a couple of nice dresses that are more than suitable for such an evening, it's tricky to know what to pack so I'm afraid I went a little overboard,' Mary said whilst laughing.

'Yes, I noticed you've brought quite a few suitcases which were heavy I might add.'

'That's what my father said.'

'Good, then that settles it. Firstly, though I'm afraid I have a small matter of important business that I need to attend to, so you're welcome to make yourself at home for a couple of hours and I shall see you later this evening,' Albert explained whilst leaning forward to give Mary a small kiss.

Albert leaving so sudden seemed a rather abrupt end to their time together Mary thought as she stood next to the Christmas tree. Perhaps like her own father the Smithers' family were never far away from work and she understood that more than anyone.

She hadn't up to now managed to work out the Smithers' line of business. After making numerous enquiries she'd discovered that they had investments in a lot of small companies; several overseas in the Far East and quite a few of them looked to be registered in mainland Europe as well as farmland over in America. One evening, she'd asked her father about Albert's business but he seemed just as confused. Eventually he told her that he believed them to be worth a small fortune.

Mary stood alone, she looked around the room again appreciating the grand decor. The house seemed quieter than back home and although it was a cold day nonetheless the sun was out and so having nothing particular to do Mary thought she would walk around the grounds for some fresh air.

She went quickly back up the main staircase which led to her room so she could change into some warmer clothes. It was as she passed along one of the further corridors which led to the back of the house, she heard some music playing which seemed to be coming from a gramophone. It was Mozart and because it was one of mother's favourite pieces she listened more intently and started to walk towards the far rooms where the music seemed to be coming from.

Suddenly the music stopped, then the strangest thing happened, the door of the room closed abruptly with a bang startling Mary. She hesitated still listening for the music. Perhaps she reasoned it was one of the housekeepers as they lived at the back of the house. She knew the Smithers' family occupied only the rooms at the front of the house. Mary listened carefully but she could not hear a sound, in fact suddenly it had become eerily quiet and Mary was all too aware that she was on her own. She shouldn't feel scared but she did.

She tried to calm herself, thinking quickly who was in the house. Albert had two brothers, Jacob the eldest brother had been cruelly killed on the front near Ypres just weeks after enlisting. Albert's other brother Giles had also fought in the last year of 1917 but thankfully had survived though sadly had lost one arm in conflict. He had emigrated a few years ago to live in Barbados and as far as Mary knew he still lived there.

Albert was too young to have fought. It seemed ironic that being born a year or two later dictated the difference between fighting or not. Generally in life, fate always decided and some matters were truly out of our hands.

Mary was still thinking about the music and its whereabouts. In the kitchens the staff probably had a fair hand and went about their business as they saw fit but in the main part of the house, the rules were very different and staff had to behave impeccably.

Feeling braver, Mary decided to walk towards her room but just as she started to move, the door opened and as Mary turned around, she saw the outline of a person who obviously didn't want to be seen as the door again was slammed shut. The only sighting that Mary could glimpse was of a woman who was fairly tall and had long auburn hair.

'Hello,' Mary managed to say, she was now rooted to the spot feeling afraid as the house was so quiet.

She waited a few moments then called again. 'Hello, is anyone there?'

There was still no response. The identity of the person behaving rudely in the room puzzled Mary. The only clue she had was the woman's hair colour, other than that Mary was none the wiser.

All the servants' quarters were a long way from this part of the house. Perhaps she consoled herself it might be one of the other guests that Albert had mentioned earlier but if that were the case, why wouldn't they introduce themselves.

Not wanting to stay a moment longer, Mary ran along the corridor and back to her room. She tried hard to put such a conundrum out of her mind but her hand was slightly shaking. She was upset and yet she didn't fully understand why. The house felt cold and unwelcoming with secrets she didn't want to know.

Perhaps it reminded her of her own childhood, her mother so cold and a father who was very kind but very busy. Mary had spent a lot of her childhood alone. If it hadn't been for members of staff like Mrs Beauvais her governess and George, Charlotte and Jimmy, then life there would have been very empty. She knew Mrs Beauvais had wanted to go back to France sooner but had waited until she thought she could leave Mary at an age she no longer needed her. The truth was that Mary needed her now more than ever.

Quickly changing into warmer clothes, Mary set off to discover the grounds of the house. Mary loved Herron Hall's grounds, her father was meticulous in how the gardens should be kept. There was an abundance of trees and plants which had been imported from all over the world.

Here at Sewter Lodge, the front gardens were immaculate yet further back from the house, Mary noticed some of the walls and pathways looked neglected and in need of repair which reflected also in the house.

Now she came to think of it, she'd noticed earlier on her arrival that the Lodge was grand and elegant where visitors could see. Elsewhere things couldn't be more different, the back of the house needed a great deal of attention and more importantly Mary thought, money spending on it.

Despite feeling out of sorts with nagging doubts about Albert, Mary enjoyed her walk. By now the sun was beginning to set as the clock tower showed just past three.

Suddenly being aware of the time, Mary started to head back. The winter light was beginning to fade and it was getting towards dusk and the wind had now stated to pick up making the late afternoon chilly. Mary had to concentrate thinking of the way back to the house. It was as she turned towards a narrow cobbled path, she got the distinct impression that someone was watching her.

Mary was not a fanciful girl by any means but as a precaution she hurried her pace. She was annoyed with herself for walking alone in the grounds of a strange house and what was becoming more obvious with each passing minute was the feeling she was lost. The Lodge never appeared any nearer even though she seemed to be walking towards it.

She stood still for a while trying to get her bearings wondering which way had she come. Now that it was completely quiet, that's when she heard the distinct sound of footsteps, and more disturbingly they sounded not too far away. She looked anxiously behind her, straining her neck to see who it was but could see no one.

Perhaps she thought after her earlier encounter in the house, her imagination was playing tricks. She tried to console herself she was being irrational. Knowing she was on her own in a strange house that was unfamiliar with and feeling lost were reasons enough to feel apprehensive to say the least.

The noise had stopped now but when Mary started her pace again, the sound could still be heard and was getting louder. For a second time that day she was left feeling perplexed and wondered who it was following her around the garden.

It was starting to get dark quickly as it does in mid winter and Mary reckoned that she was still a good five minutes walk from the house. Managing a half run, Mary started to panic, there was no one else around to ask directions. Then to her utter relief she spotted the bridge where she had first stated her walk. Five minutes seemed to be a reasonable time she thought to make it back. Mary however wasn't totally confident she could beat the person behind her, a thought that made her feel even more anxious.

'Who are you?' she demanded. 'Stop this tomfoolery at once.'

Mary was truly scared by now and her heart beat quickly. There was still no answer only the sound of stillness. The only option she had, was to make a run to the house. She took a deep breath, she felt sure she could hear somebody behind her but by now she was too scared to look back in case it slowed her pace. Mary started to run but whoever it was, was quickly behind her. Mary's frame was only slight and thankfully she was relatively fit so she knew she could run fast if needed.

She upped her pace, her breath making patterns from the cold evening. Her lungs were hurting but she knew she couldn't stop. Whoever was behind, wasn't going to give up.

Mary could at last see the entrance of the Lodge as it came into distance and felt some relief. As her feet made a crunching sound on the drive she knew she was safe but perhaps as she told herself, only for now. Just as she entered the main entrance, she heard somebody laughing, which was loud enough for her to hear, suggesting that whoever it was, they still were not far away. Breathing loudly, with her hair covering her face, Mary looked completely different from the girl who had arrived at the Lodge hours earlier. She took deep breaths as she tried to compose herself as it wouldn't bode well for her to be seen in such a state.

She needed to be on her guard and certainly didn't want Albert to see any weakness in her. Her father had always taught her to be strong even if you didn't feel it. Mary felt certain there was no mistaking someone had been there trying to scare her. Any doubts were confirmed when she heard the distinct sound of a car's engine starting and rolling down the gravelled drive. But when she turned around, she saw no vehicle.

It could have been that maybe the car was leaving from the side of the house. Mary was very observant and remembered the small drive she'd seen earlier that led to the back of the Lodge. She knew someone had been trying to frighten her and thought it no coincidence that she'd been followed in the grounds and then heard the sound of the car leaving the house, let alone the mystery of the music from the room from earlier. Maybe she should tell George but decided for now to keep her fears to herself.

Mary was still preoccupied by her own thoughts and therefore was most surprised to see Albert standing by the doorway of the drawing room. He seemed slightly nervous she noticed. Normally his hair was worn slicked back from his face but now it looked untidy as though he'd been in a rush to get somewhere.

'Did you enjoy your stroll Mary?' he enquired as he lit his cigarette. 'Do you smoke?'

'No, it's not something I care about,' Mary said her voice slightly shaking.

'Do you mind?'

'Not at all, it doesn't bother me but I'm afraid my father detests the habit.'

Mary watched as Albert put the cigarette in his mouth and slowly inhaled as if deep in thought. She was just about to tell him about her strange encounters but something instinctively told her not to, so instead she bit her lip after all in the cold light of day there was nothing really to tell. She had seen no one yet she knew somebody had been trying to scare her and if truth be known they certainly had.

'I'll go and change now and return to my room.'

Mary went quickly to her room and once upstairs as she was changing her clothes, she felt an uneasy feeling. There was something not quite right about Sewter Lodge and yet there was nothing Mary could put her finger on and it troubled her.

The house itself was grand and impressive yet parts also neglected. The woman who still remained anonymous with auburn hair puzzled her and knowing that she had been followed outside by somebody who wanted to scare her and then hearing the strange laughter. Lastly, the car which had suddenly sped off yet not down the main drive. Mary wasn't enjoying her visit and the situation didn't add up, it was as though she was missing something but couldn't think for the life of her what it was.

Mary Green was elegant at the best of times yet tonight she looked exquisite. She'd dressed in a purple velvet dress which was complemented by a white silk shawl that had pearls hand sewn on the fabric. She simply looked faultless. Albert looked up from his seat as she entered the room, smiled and looked pleased.

Albert's family certainly knew how to entertain and the table looked magnificent with holly wreaths and candles carefully placed. Although Mary had been in the room earlier that day, now as night time had come, it looked even grander. Albert was a courteous man and immediately made the obligatory introductions.

'Mary, you look simply divine. May I introduce Charles and Edith Bickerstaff and Jacob and Penelope Edmunds.'

Albert gestured to the two couples on the far right of the table. Mary greeted the two women but was disappointed to see that both Edith and Penelope were brunettes and sadly had not one strand of auburn hair between them. When she checked again both women looked quite petite whereas the woman she had seen earlier was quite tall.

'It's lovely to meet you Mary, Albert has been telling us that you live far away, in the north of the country near Whitby, we've never been there but have heard it's a quaint little fishing village,' Edith said politely.

Mary was very proud of her home and the surrounding villages and wished more people would visit as they would be surprised by the beauty of the area.

'Yes, we're on the North Yorkshire moors, it's a beautiful spot but it can be quite rugged on the moorlands and prone to sea frets and days of rain in winter,' Mary said honestly.

'How charming, we once went as far as Harrogate, didn't we Jacob, a lovely cake shop, Betty's ... that's the name I believe it opened a couple of years ago, was it 1919?'

'Yes, that's right... beautiful piece of Victoria Sponge Cake we had, apparently they wanted to make the place rather similar to the coffee houses in Switzerland,' Jacob said and nodded in agreement acknowledging Mary.

'Harrogate is very pretty as is most of North Yorkshire,' Mary chirped. 'I've been telling Albert that he simply must visit the area more.'

'Well I have a very good reason now, don't I,' Albert said rather charmingly.

'I say, Pens, didn't Jim's sons go there, catholic family they are... what the devil was the school called?'

'Ampleforth, that's the school's name apparently it's a damned good school by all accounts,' Penelope responded enthusiastically glad she knew something about the area.

'Absolutely,' Mary said determined to defend her lovely part of the country. 'I myself had a governess but some of daddy's friends' sons went there and have good careers in local law firms.'

Mary fidgeted in her chair, it seemed tonight could be a long laborious evening. She glanced across the table towards Albert who seemed just as uneasy. It was as though he had other things on his mind.

'Albert tells us your father owns some of the textile mills in a place called Halifax, I bet business must have boomed with the sale of auxiliary uniforms, why David must have made a small fortune, that's the funny thing with the war, be in the right place and make a bloody fortune out of it, luck I say,' Charles said rather too loudly as he had one of those voices that could not speak quietly.

Mary was taken aback by Charles' forthright manner. It was true her father had seen production increase at a tremendous rate as the scramble for uniforms became paramount during war times. Her father had also given a lot of money to families still suffering from the aftermath of such times. He was no doubt a good business man but to call him ruthless was simply not right and it made Mary feel uncomfortable.

She smiled wanting to talk no more about her father's fortunes. He had always taught her to be both humble and grateful. Here she didn't want to be David Green's daughter, she wanted to be just herself.

'Your father is talented in business, to that I have no doubt,' James Smithers said.

This was the first time that James had spoken. He was an older version of his son in every way from the same swept back hair to his square jaw line. Like Albert he seemed to rarely smile and seemed preoccupied also like his son.

'I think so but daddy's father, my grandfather was a wonderful man,' Mary said keen to steer the conversation from business. 'He travelled extensively sometimes for business but mostly just for fun. Do you like travelling?'

As soon as Mary's question was asked, she noticed James glance at his son and an awkwardness appeared between them.

'Yes, we have travelled frequently, mostly around Europe,' James answered curtly.

It was now Henrietta's turn to speak, Albert's mother. She was extremely elegant with long blond hair, she reminded Mary of the women she'd met in Europe when travelling. Although she'd lived in England a long time, her Russian accent was still strong and seemed to soften only when she asked one of the servants for some more wine to be served.

Mary got the feeling that both Albert's parents had no feeling or sentiment for her and as the conversation carried on through the evening, she felt very much an outsider. She hadn't expected any fuss but the lack of warmth made Mary feel disappointed by the Smithers' family.

In fact, when Mary had politely enquired about their other son Giles, Henrietta had fair snarled at her, and Mary soon got the impression not to ask any personal questions which left Mary wondering just what to talk about.

Thankfully Charles seemed to have a lot to say for himself so there were no voids in conversation. As the evening drew to a close Mary felt relieved when at last she and Albert were excused from the table.

'You look beautiful tonight Mary,' Albert said as he slipped his arm through hers. 'Purple really suits you and your shawl is exquisite.'

'Thank you, it was very pleasant and the meal was lovely,' Mary said truthfully as the food had tasted delicious.

They walked slowly along the corridor to the foot of the main stairs.

'Mary,' Albert spoke gently. 'What is it?' Mary replied. Mary turned around to find Albert bent on his knees holding a ring on his lap. Mary couldn't believe this was happening, it felt almost absurd and as far as she was concerned it was far too soon to make such a commitment. There was however little else she could do except stand politely next to Albert and hope and pray for the best and in some ways she knew there and then that she didn't have a choice.

'I've already taken the liberty of asking both of our fathers. Would you give me the pleasure of taking my hand in marriage and become my wife?'

Mary was speechless, she had never been a romantic girl but Albert's proposal seemed almost clinical. A nasty thought dawned on her that her parents had been very much part of these shenanigans and in some ways, it brought home to her that when it came to it, a daughter was only an expensive bargaining tool.

Mary felt powerless and there was nothing she could do, she had always known she couldn't marry for love but nevertheless a sadness filled her that she couldn't describe. The world she belonged to with all its glamour, money and power, now didn't seem so attractive. Mary had seen couples from ordinary backgrounds courting and it bore no likeness to this. Something in her heart snapped, she closed her eyes and could see Jimmy's face.

Albert was waiting for an answer and she knew she had to say something. She wanted to say she needed time but knew she couldn't.

'Yes, Albert I would very much like to be your wife,' she said allowing herself a slight smile but as soon as she answered she knew it was a big mistake.

Albert got up from his bended knee and was smiling at her. He seemed genuinely pleased or was it a relief, Mary couldn't quite decide and in some ways, she didn't want to, either way it was irrelevant as at least now a decision had been made and she just would have to hope that Albert would prove to be a good husband. Like any new bride to be she would never know until it was too late.

'Let's go back and share the good news,' Albert said holding Mary's hand tightly and leading her back to the drawing room where the people had moved into.

'Yes, that would be nice.'

'Would you like to telephone your parents? Though the line to the north may not work this time of night.'

Albert was trying to be kind towards her and Mary appreciated that.

'Yes, my mother will be particularly very pleased I would imagine,' Mary enthused wanting to sound more excited than she actually felt, she knew at least she had to pretend to be pleased.

'And of course your father,' Albert said awkwardly.

'Yes of course.'

Mary knew her mother would be most pleased, she had wanted her to marry for wealth and in Albert she had the perfect match.

As the couple went back into the drawing room there was already a toast waiting for them.

'Congratulations Albert and Mary and we all drink to a long and prosperous marriage,' James Smithers announced. 'Here, here,' came a chorus from Henrietta and her guests.

There was no turning back and Mary knew it, just by saying yes, the promise was sealed not to be broken and she knew there and then she'd just made the deal of all deals. Mary smiled at her guests and Albert, after all she thought what else could she do.

As George drove Mary back north to Herron Hall the following day, this gave Mary time to reflect on her visit and many thoughts crossed her mind from the proposal and the implications that brought not just for herself but also her family.

'Thank you for your support yesterday, it was very nice of you to congratulate us,' Mary said.'

'You know I've always wanted you to be happy. I've worked for your father for many years. Your father and particularly your mother will be very pleased,' George replied trying to sound enthusiastic but Mary sensed a sadness in his manner.

'Are you pleased with the news?' Mary asked cautiously not wanting him to answer. 'I mean really...pleased?'

'Well, it's not up to me to say,' George said honestly. 'But both your families seem matched in every way.'

'If truth be known, Albert perplexes me?' Mary said. 'What do you make of him?'

'Well, Albert is a very eligible bachelor and most young ladies in your position would feel rather pleased with themselves.'

'So why do I feel so uneasy?' Mary asked trying to sound happier than she felt.

'Well... firstly, you don't really know Albert and neither does he know you.'

'Do you think he will give me the run around?'

Mary would have never asked such direct questions to her parents but with George she felt different. George was almost family and the almost part made him her friend.

'You already know the answer to that. A man like Albert...well who's to say,' George said honestly.

He glanced at Mary but knew he hadn't offended her. Mary was a smart girl and he was pleased she could talk to him. Her own mother was cold and her father who loved her dearly was a busy man and after that Mary had no one else she could confide in.

'I wish I could talk to my mother. I have tried to talk about Albert and my reservations but she won't hear a bad word against him,' Mary said sadly. 'She likes him rather too much.'

George nodded sympathetically. 'I've mentioned to David on more than one occasion my reservations about Albert but he tells me your mother is quite taken by him.'

'That's what worries me, it's usually mummy who gets her own way.'

Mary tried to busy herself by looking at the frost on the trees as the car quickly passed by. Inside the car felt warm and she wanted to go to sleep but her visit to Sewter Lodge had left her feeling uneasy and she could not feel any joy about her new situation, only a nervousness that she was now part of something that she knew nothing about and sadly she felt she didn't want to.

'What am I going to do George? How can I get out of this marriage. I feel my fate is doomed, I know Albert is completely wrong for me and will never make me happy.'

'I have no influence over your mother, Bella certainly won't listen to me,' George replied honestly. 'I've always been close to your father, I can only talk to him.'

Mary smiled as she thought of her mother and Jimmy. Her mother had never been too keen on him nor George. She liked Charlotte who managed the staff for her. Charlotte had an easy going manner and was eager to please. Traits that her mother always admired in people, it made her feel important.

'There must be something I can do?' Mary said her voice a little shaky from her visit and the shock of now being engaged to a man she didn't really know. 'Perhaps I can call the engagement off.'

'Perhaps but I doubt that. Let's see what happens,' George said kindly. 'I know things don't look too good but don't do anything hasty.'

Mary decided that once home she would discuss these doubts with her father. But the more she thought about the matter, it left her more confused, what was it that she could actually say was wrong with Albert. On the face of it, he appeared kind, attentive, good looking and wealthy. If she was to say to her father he was a ladies' man. Her father would just laugh, half the men he knew were. She couldn't quite put her finger on exactly what the problem was but everything in her told her that Albert Smithers was a bad man.

As the journey went on however and they neared home, Mary had the feeling of queasiness which was starting to grow to a terrible feeling of dread so much so that she only hoped for her parents' sake she could get through the wedding, let alone the marriage.

# Chapter 5

'There's so much to arrange,' Bella announced excitedly as she twisted her hair, a habit she had when something was bothering her.

'Yes, father's very excited,' Mary said trying to reassure her mother.

'Albert is far more connected to society than we are,' her mother said looking very pleased with herself.

Mary nodded. 'I know you think Albert is a very good husband but... I guess I'm still a little apprehensive.'

She'd tried over the last few weeks to convince her parents that Albert was not the best choice for a husband. Her father had tried to listen and at one point had been willing to call a halt to the wedding. Her mother however wouldn't hear of such nonsense as she called it. She'd repeatedly told Mary that in no uncertain terms could she call the wedding off. As far as she was concerned, Albert was a perfect husband.

'I'm still having doubts about Albert, you know that to be true.'

'It's completely natural to have reservations. Albert I know is a very good match, and I honestly think you should feel happy,' her mother said impatiently. 'You might not get an offer like this again.'

'But I'm not ready for this,' Mary insisted.

'No bride ever really is darling,' Bella said.

Mary sighed, it was pointless trying to talk about Albert with her mother. There really was no discussion.

'I wish I didn't have to go through with it.'

'The decision has been made Mary, you have a duty to both your father and myself.'

It was a cold bleak winter that year and the wind brought heavy snows which kept Mary bolted indoors for the good part of January. At last winter passed and the warmer winds blew in from the sea and the appearance of the landscape changed making it look softer and full of life after the snow and ice.

Soon spring gave way to summer and the heathers on the moors blossomed and changed colours. As it did so, a new excitement seemed to fill every corner of Herron Hall that is of course for everyone except Mary.

Her parents it seemed were determined to make the wedding one that was going to be both grand and worthy of their only daughter.

When it came to organising such occasions there was nobody better than Bella Green. No expense had been spared and Herron Hall looked even more opulent. New furnishings and fabrics were ordered in abundance for the many rooms around the house. Gardeners worked almost round the clock and as the day neared there was hardly a flower or leaf out of place.

Caterers and exquisite food had been ordered from London and Mary felt sure that even the best hotels in London would have struggled to serve such fine food.

From time to time over those months Mary and Albert had met each other mostly at Albert's home, Sewter Lodge in Sussex. Naturally Mary had been on her guard from her previous encounters. She'd purposefully looked for the woman with auburn hair but had never seen her.

She had told no one about the strange events but as a precaution she had purposely not made her visits long. Mary however was relieved that she had seen nothing untoward at the Lodge to cause her concern and consequently she soon put the matter to the back of her mind as she became more and more involved with the preparations of the wedding.

Mary still had many doubts about the wedding and Albert concerned her. The more she got to know him the more she cared less. He showed her little affection and always seemed preoccupied. Sometimes in the evenings he would work late in his father's office writing letters.

It was one such evening that Mary happened to catch the tail end of a telephone conversation. Albert was unaware that Mary was eavesdropping. As luck would have it, Albert spoke loud enough for Mary to hear some of the dialogue and she distinctly heard the subject of money mentioned for substantial amounts. This alarmed Mary to think of such vast sums of money being talked about and not surprisingly this worried her.

Now she came to think of it, Albert himself never appeared to have any money upon his person. This led her to think that throughout the few months she'd known Albert there had never been any generous gifts for her despite his continuous boasting of wealth which he often mentioned in conversation.

She had also presumed that as a couple after they were married, they would live in the south in Albert's home county of Sussex and therefore was most surprised when Albert had made it clear that he wanted to live in the empty Lodge in Herron Hall's grounds.

Mary was even more taken aback by her parents' reaction as they both seemed over the moon by this decision, whereas she thought they would have wanted her to live in the south.

Mary had wondered on more than one occasion from what she had seen and sometimes by the way Albert behaved if his family were rather short of money. Albert frequently told her about their vast amounts of investments overseas but Mary knew enough about business to know this wasn't a secure world and wondered if they had lost money from poor business decisions. One day she discussed her concerns with her father who only seemed to dismiss the idea of Albert being poor or falling on hard times as being ridiculous.

'Really Mary you worry far too much, it's not as though you will be on the bread line for heavens sake,' her father said. 'Besides you have your own money.'

'But father... once I'm married to Albert he will take all that money.'

'Your mother really wouldn't like me discussing such matters,' her father paused. 'Most of our wealth is still in my name. Yes, you have some wealth, but at the moment unless I pass away and I have no intention of doing so yet, then not much of the estate is yours yet.'

Her father was a sensible man and maybe although he wouldn't say it out loud, he too didn't trust Albert. If he didn't, he did right Mary thought to herself.

'But I really do believe Albert has no money of his own,' Mary replied.

'Then neither do you.'

'Well why does Albert want to marry me then? '

'Perhaps it's for love.'

Both her father and Mary looked at each other and smiled. They both knew this wasn't true, the household had always been ruled by her mother, both knew better than to question the status quo, it's just the way things were.

Mary decided there and then never to bring up the subject of Albert Smithers again as much not to hurt her father's feelings and to upset herself. She still felt strong reservations about the union and although she acted very polite around Albert, everything in her told her this was not a man she could trust but perhaps she reassured herself that what was to be expected of a husband.

# Chapter 6

'Mary you only have less than twenty minutes before we walk to the car my dear, do get a move on after all we don't want to be late that would be terrible for your own wedding,' her mother said as she opened the door and saw her daughter standing with three servants and the dressmaker who had carefully sewn by hand Mary's wedding dress.

The dress was beautiful with carefully placed pearls adding to its elegance. Though simple in design, it had beautiful embroidery with silver thread weaved in and out of loose lace.

'You look beautiful my dear. You make a lovely bride,' Bella said looking pleased.

Mary allowed herself a little smile. The dress was very elegant but was wasted on Mary. The truth was she didn't really care how she looked. Albert had in fairness been very kind of late to her but she hadn't changed her mind about him one bit. She doubted she ever would.

Jimmy had visited the Hall recently to see his parents. She had spent an afternoon with him riding on the moors. Both Mary and Jimmy were accomplished riders and their time had been made extra special by the afternoon's weather being particularly mild. Jimmy was fun and easy company everything Albert wasn't. There had been a special moment between them when they'd walked back to the Hall from the stables. Jimmy had taken hold of Mary's hand in an innocent friendly way. The tingle from his skin had been so nice and to feel his touch. It reminded Mary what it felt like to be in love with someone.

'Yes, it's a very beautiful dress and surprisingly easy to wear,' Mary said pushing all thoughts of Jimmy away as she sadly looked into the mirror.

'As you know, we have family arriving from America and some of your father's friends from the city,' Bella said, her hands still flattening any crumples in the dress. 'Jimmy is also here.'

Bella cast Mary a sharp glance. 'He's staying at the Lodge. I know you enjoyed seeing him recently but Mary you have to hide your feelings for him.'

'Jimmy is here,' Mary blurted out feeling slightly better for hearing such good news.

'I know you're close to George and treated Jimmy as something of an older brother but really Mary you must now never think of him as anything more, he's part of your past.'

'I know...it's just I would love to talk to him, if only... '

'Life has no time for if only, besides Jimmy is not our sort and you know that.'

'No quite, you've made me only too aware,' Mary said in an ungracious voice.

'Well, come now,' Bella said standing to her feet, 'It's time Mary, you look truly wonderful, a beautiful bride. Come dear, the car is waiting,' Bella said more to herself than Mary whilst making sure they had everything before leaving the room.

'I'm going out of Herron Hall as a single woman and when I come back in a fortnight I will be a married woman,' Mary said nervously.

'Being married will suit you Mary and I think your life is about to change,' her mother said whilst helping her down the stairs making sure her veil was still neatly in place.

The church was just outside Herron Hall, although small it was just big enough to hold the wedding. Technically David owned and maintained the church, vicarage and grounds but a few years ago, rather generously he'd donated the church and the surrounding parish hall and fields to the local parishioners which had undoubtedly won him a few favours with local farmers and villagers alike.

David was always shrewd in matters of business and knew that a small favour given would result in a big one to ask in return. It was a belief that had served him well in his life and Mary was quickly learning the valuable lesson that hard work and patience in life generally paid off. David was well liked around the village and surrounding area as well as Mary. People were treated fairly and made to feel part of the estate and it was because of this that people worked hard for David.

As Mary walked up the narrow cobbled path to the church she could hear the organ playing. She peered through the church doors and could see what her mother deemed to be the great and good of society. The congregation was heavily loaded on her mother's side with a few aristocrats dotted in between the guests.

Her father's family had travelled from America and some of the wealthy from the east coast had made the long journey for the wedding. With a few locals and parishioners seated in between, Mary's half of the church looked respectable and refined. She knew her father would be pleased as this would allow David's friends in Fleet Street to make the notices that week. Her mother had repeatedly told Mary that a wedding of this pedigree should certainly make the papers.

By contrast, the other half of the church on the Smithers' side looked far less grand. Albert's parents and a few acquaintances that Mary knew seemed out of place with the other selection of people who had been invited. Mary cast an eye around the congregation. She couldn't help but think that maybe this was an insight into the real Albert Smithers.

Mary often wondered about Albert's family and it caused her concern but before her thoughts had time to rest, she found herself facing the alter.

The ceremony itself was faultless and passed so quickly that the next thing Mary knew she was walking back down the aisle with Albert as husband and wife. She hadn't wanted this marriage but now at least the wedding ceremony was over.

Mary felt slightly more relaxed and she made time to smile at guests on both sides, it was then right at the back of the church that Mary noticed a woman on her own.

The woman wore a large purple hat but it was her hair that most caught Mary's attention. The woman had exactly the same auburn coloured hair just like the woman from Sewter Lodge who had scared Mary so much from her first visit there. Mary instinctively knew that this had to be the same woman.

She checked along the aisles of the church again to see if she was related somehow to the other guests but it was obvious to Mary that she was definitely on her own.

To confirm her suspicions as Mary passed her, the woman lowered her hat as though she was determined not to let Mary see her face. The same uneasiness came over Mary as before when she had first encountered her. She knew the woman whoever she was would be up to no good. She glanced at Albert but he gave the woman no attention. Perhaps Mary thought, she was a servant or housekeeper that had worked for Albert's family at some point. This however did not explain the woman's reluctance to introduce herself.

As the church bells rang, Mary made a mental note to ask Albert who the particular guest was but the following day as Mary boarded the train destined for Victoria Station by then she had a hundred things on her mind and somehow auburn hair for now seemed far less important.

Their journey was firstly to London and then onwards to the south west coast to Southampton, and from then on they would head to the French port of Caen and finally to Le Touquet in northern France. It was here at the glitzy seaside resort where they would spend their honeymoon. Even though Mary had travelled often to France she had never been to Le Touquet but the coast itself was beautiful and remained a very special place in her heart. How she wished she was coming here married to Jimmy and not as Mrs. Smithers, a name she knew no matter how many times she heard, she would never accept. Herron Hall and it's safety were beginning to feel a long way off.

# Chapter 7

When the final guests of the wedding had left, David Green allowed himself a long sigh. He was delighted that the day had been a success. Although Bella had arranged the grandiose touches to the wedding, it was David along with several of the senior staff that had made sure down to the last detail that everything had gone according to plan.

With only a few months to organise such a big event, David had taken a keen interest in the Smithers' family in order to try to make the wedding convivial to both families. Bella was keen for her daughter to marry well but although David had gone along with such proceedings, he felt a greater sense of responsibility for his only daughter. Mary reminded him so much of himself and he felt an overriding obligation to protect her.

In reality after those few months of planning he now saw Albert Smithers as a rather foolish man but hoped he would become with time and much guidance, a very good husband to Mary. Deep in his heart though, he knew no man whoever they were, would ever seem good enough for her and therefore Albert seemed the best of a bad lot.

David himself was a quiet thoughtful man and in the past, he'd had several business dealings with James, Albert's father but of late he'd heard one or two rumours about the financial affairs of both Albert and James. It was not a matter that bothered him too much. In fairness, Mary had enough money of her own for her to have married a pauper and never worry about finance. David however had to admit to himself that he was more worried about Albert somehow managing to control all of Mary's money not that much of the business at the moment was legally documented in her name. It still however was a concern just as it was for most fathers but in Mary's case, she was sole heir to a vast fortune.

On several occasions, he had voiced his concerns to Bella but she didn't seem to be at all worried about Albert. Bella had always thought that he'd make an ideal husband for Mary. As David stood in his study thinking about his daughter and son in law, Bella came into the room interrupting his thoughts.

'It was such a beautiful wedding David, everybody that came had only the nicest of comments. Mary looked so beautiful and they make such a wonderful couple, they looked so lovely together, don't you think?' Bella commented smiling at David who looked less than convinced.

'Yes, it was very nice but there was a lot to organise for such a big society wedding,' David caught his wife's glance.

'But we did it so well for Mary.'

'Still it was a big day for all of us. Now that the world is getting smaller and cars seem common place, it seems that everything has to be bigger and better than when we married.'

David looked at his wife and proceeded to sit.

'Well times move on David, you have to be adaptable that's what the government is always telling us.'

'Of course, ... it still would have been nice to have had in retrospect a little more time for all the preparations Bella, after all,' he smiled choosing his words carefully. 'I am still worried in some ways that they hardly know each other, of course I've no doubt that Albert is a lovely young man but you said only last year that his father had some dubious dealings with a man from Paris you mentioned?' David didn't want to appear too direct.

David studied his wife's reaction, he had always if truth be known, felt inferior to her and although he appeared more confident, he knew better than to ignore his wife. Her blue blood seemed to have given her have an icy manner which he had never quite understood and hoped would mellow with age but she'd never changed.

'I have to say, I think they will be very happy together David, you have to give them time. Albert is a little older than Mary but he's got a head for business and we just need to get to know him,' Bella said more to herself than David. This was true and David knew that there was little else to say but he thought he ought to say it any way.

'That's the point Bella, I don't think in many ways he is at all suitable for Mary, I've had my doubts from the start as you know but I've kept them very much to myself. Mary as we both know is sole heir to a lot of money.'

David paused but he had come this far and wanted his view point heard. 'I hate to admit this but I don't really know anything about Albert and it would be a tragedy if there was something that perhaps came out later now that they are married.'

Bella looked startled by David's comments. 'You worry far too much, I trust Albert and I think Mary is sweet on him.'

Bella was a little ruffled now and wondered how long this conversation would keep going.

'Do you know Bella, neither Albert or his family have offered one penny towards the wedding, of course we wouldn't take a dime but that's not the point Bella and you know that.'

David was getting annoyed by now and could see that he wasn't going to convince his wife to see his point of view. He got up from his seat and paced backwards and forwards passing the fireplace. David knew there was something that wasn't quite right and the more he'd thought about Albert, sense told him that he should have never rushed Mary into marriage. David felt a burning desire to protect his daughter and if that meant ruffling a few feathers then he'd do it. He felt helpless as he knew that he'd been pushed by Bella to choose Albert. It was Bella who had persuaded Albert to be invited to the Ball. David was such a careful man normally and he should not have listened to his wife. Bella on this matter had been more persistent than ever.

'Bella if there's something you need to tell me, I want to know?' David asked hoping his wife would see sense.

'David, what's done's done and I simply won't hear any more on the matter.'

'But...'

'No David, they're married now, we leave it to them,' Bella said, her manner cold.

'It's settled then.'

David drifted into his American accent which Bella knew was always more pronounced when he felt agitated. Bella also knew that she would say no more on the matter but by David's anxiousness, he'd already told her more than she needed to.

David was drifting back to his own thoughts and bitterly regretted such a union to take place. So desperate he'd been to marry his daughter off that he'd taken his eye off the ball and as David knew that old adage, act in haste repent at leisure, were wise words for a reason. David was more than aware that to leave matters as they were was wrong but as he drained the last bit of brandy from his glass, he thought that he would slowly start to think of a plan. He would treat this just as he did in business and put his ideas forward. What he needed was time to consider this matter carefully.

David did nothing for a few days as he was still mainly dealing with the aftermath of the wedding and making sure some semblance came back to the Hall and its workings. Slowly however, like most good plans one started to formulate in his head and by the Friday of that week, David picked up the telephone to contact the one person that he could trust.

# Chapter 8

The train by now had pulled into a small station which seemed poorly lit for the time of night. A few passengers entered the train which was running late. Sophie offered Emily a piece of fudge from her tin box which she gratefully accepted.

'What did David do? He must have been beside himself and regretting the wedding?' Sophie asked taking the tin and putting it on the edge of the table.

'Well David of course was a quiet man but he had a brother who was much younger than him and it just so happened that his younger brother was himself living in London after recently moving from a law firm in Boston. At the time, he lived just outside the city in a grand house and commuted by train for his work.'

'He sounds very wealthy?'

'Yes,' Emily answered. 'He was and very connected as well. David assumed correctly that Albert and his brother would mix in similar circles. The difference between the two men was that Edward was naturally gifted and after studying at Oxford, he then trained to be a solicitor and would have taken his bar exams to become a barrister but was quickly head hunted by a law firm back home in America. He soon rose the ranks to become a senior partner. It was then an opportunity came about to work in London.

It was a shrewd move which opened many doors and Edward was easily accepted in most of the city's gentlemen's clubs.'

Emily helped herself to another fudge which she ate slower this time allowing it to melt in her mouth whilst giving her time to think. She looked through the window of the train, it was now virtually dark. They seemed to be travelling much slower than she had expected and the train was now running late. Emily took a sip of her tea and continued with her story.

'That was the day that David arranged to meet Edward in Leeds hoping that he could shed some light on Albert Smithers and maybe lay some of David's uncertainties to rest. David often went there for work. He hoped Bella would just presume he was going to Leeds for business. He didn't want to alarm her about Albert especially if his worries proved to be unfounded, he knew better than to cause a fuss when there was probably nothing to the story.

Bella tended to worry and David felt an overwhelming sense of guilt because at the end of the day, it was after all his own fault, he'd allowed Mary to marry Albert. Not to have done his homework was a school boy error and one that may prove to cost him dearly.

Leeds station is a world away from Kings Cross in London. Edward still couldn't get used to how small it was in comparison. Edward Green was a good looking man and when he smiled it made him more so. He stood in his smart overcoat waiting for David. He reminisced to their childhood and couldn't help thinking how different both brothers were.

Edward had a nonchalant approach to life, unlike David who was very focused. Edward tended to take life at a much slower pace than his brother a gift that David admired. Both brothers though worked hard and were men of principle and had a kindness that showed in their face.

David was pleased he could see more of his brother now that he lived in England and hoped for now he wouldn't return to America.

'Oh Edward, thank goodness you've come, it's so good to see you,' David said and grabbed Edward giving him a brotherly slap on the back. David was very fond of Edward, though he still thought of him as being far younger than himself. It was only eight years but in reality the gap always seemed more.

'Great to see you big brother,' Edward said.

'Thanks for coming today as I know I've not given you much notice,' David smiled. 'Apologies as I daren't invite you back home. You see there's some nasty business I want to discuss and it's important not be rumbled by Bella.'

'Right I see,' Edward hesitated now concerned by the news. 'Whatever it is, I know it's making you worried and that worries me.'

'Well, Bella's a bit of a stick in the mud and wouldn't approve of what I'm about to ask.'

David didn't want to sound too anxious and tried to change the subject.

'How's Verity and the twins, it was lovely to see them at the wedding, gorgeous as ever?'

'They're fine, not so much gorgeous but I think the right word is mischievous as ever.'

'It's been too long in between visits, you simply must come back to Herron Hall with Verity,' David said wishing that he could see his brother for longer.

'Yes, we need to meet more often. Verity insists you visit us in Sussex. You must come down to see George and Beatrice.'

Edward hadn't changed one bit and family life obviously suited him. George and Beatrice were just three and Edward had joked that at least by having twins, he'd got fatherhood out of the way in one go.

'Yes, we'd love to come for a few days and I simply adore George and Beatrice, though I'm sure they're a handful.' David laughed as his brother nodded in agreement. 'Edward, I thought we could have lunch at Simones, they serve a delicious menu worthy of coming all the way up to Leeds and have a rather delicious light tea. I've even took the liberty of reserving a table that will allow us some privacy. By four o 'clock though, I must be getting back. But you'll be pleased to know you're booked into the hotel for tonight which by all accounts is rather nice.'

Edward smiled wondering just what was bothering David so much. He'd always thought of him as calm and not the sort of man to be easily ruffled. He'd never cared for

Bella and thought her to be cold and manipulating. Over the years, despite his reservations, Edward acknowledged that David seemed happy enough and knew he loved his daughter Mary who in Edward's opinion seemed a miniature version of her father. Edward was fond of his niece who had a cheerful, happy disposition.

Simones was a grand restaurant that was very popular. Edward appreciated that it wasn't too far a walk from the train station. The building by the looks of things had recently been refurbished in a new style called Art Deco which was all the rage. As promised, David had reserved a table at the back of the restaurant, perfectly positioned, making it unlikely that anyone would eavesdrop on their conversation.

'So, what is it that's bothering you David? I must say it's not like you to be so agitated and wanting advice from your younger sibling,' Edward laughed, he had always been the joker of the two. 'Albert Smithers is not particularly liked but as far as I know on paper, he's as clean as a whistle. He's a lady's man through and through and I think he will give poor Mary the go around but it's not enough to hold some terrible grudge David,' Edward said trying to reassure his brother.

'Yes, I know that,' David acknowledged. 'But are you sure you have no information; there must be some dirt on him, I can feel it, call it intuition. I don't think the Smithers' family for one have the money that Bella thinks they have and even Mary I know has had some reservations though in fairness, poor girl, she married him to please me and more importantly Bella.'

Edward was right in thinking David didn't approve of Albert Smithers and had not really wanted the wedding to go ahead. He knew his brother wanted some information about Albert or his father. Sensing this he thought it best to tell him something as he hated to see his brother so upset.

'Well... now I come to think of it, there is something... it may of course be nothing, it's just I was privy to a conversation at work a few weeks ago.'

'Yes, go on?' David said his eyes lightning up.

'As you know we deal with a lot of contracts from overseas. As we got talking, Albert's name came up several times regarding certain companies in mainland Europe. The companies that were mentioned I might add were not our clients but more of... a dubious nature shall we say. Though such an association is not a crime David,' Edward said choosing his words carefully.

'Perhaps not but as I've recently found out, Albert and his father are not well liked in some circles.'

David looked thoughtful. He didn't like what he was hearing, he knew Edward was trying to help but this was perhaps the news he didn't want to hear. He looked down at his sandwiches that had been carefully presented, he usually had a good appetite but suddenly it had somewhat faded and a deep regret filled his mind. He finished his glass of port with thoughts of going home.

It was getting near the end of the afternoon and David wanted to enjoy his brother's company so for the rest of the time they had, they talked about other things. David seemed to relax but Edward knew he was still worried and on a mission to help his daughter. As they walked out of the smart restaurant, he tapped his brother on the shoulder.

'Look David. I'll tell you what I'll have a word with a friend of mine he's an Inspector for the London Met,' Edward said his eyes now twinkling. 'In fact you also know him.'

'Who?' David looked surprised.

Edward smiled to himself, David may be smarter in business than him but in ordinary day to day matters he had a tendency not to think practically. 'You're forgetting young Jimmy, George and Charlotte's son.'

'Gosh, how could I have forgotten. Jimmy of course, why didn't I think of him. In fact, I've mentioned to George on a few occasions my nagging doubts about Albert?'

'Well think no more about it. When I get back home, I'll contact him as soon as possible and besides Mary's always had a soft spot for him so she'll be more than happy to confide any fears.'

'Yes, of course,' David said smiling at last. 'I'll have a word with George, I doubt if Charlotte would tell Bella, I'm sure she knows to keep quiet, There's probably nothing more to the story but to tell the truth Edward, I'm very suspicious of Albert and right now Mary is miles away in France. I just pray she'll be alright,' David acknowledged.

'Mary is tougher than she looks.'

'Promise me she'll be alright Edward, if anything should happen to her... I'd feel terrible. This is all my fault.'

'Nonsense David, I'm sure you're letting your imagination run away. Albert won't hurt Mary.'

'Yes, I hope you're right.' David rubbed his forehead. 'I guess I'm more tired than I thought, you know after the wedding, that's all.'

'Yes, but nevertheless I'll have a word with Jimmy,' Edward said. 'I owe him a drink after all, I know his parents have worked for you for many years. Why, I feel I know them too from my visits. I can't believe Jimmy's a man now, I can still remember him chasing Mary round the gardens and that doesn't seem a minute ago.'

David looked at his brother and laughed.

'Yes, he was a bit of a rascal then, perfect for catching criminals I'd say.'

David sometimes felt that Edward wasn't as hard working as himself but deep in his heart he knew Edward wouldn't let him down.

'You will contact him, won't you?' David asked again, his voice quite desperate.

'You have my word.'

'Oh, thank you, in some ways it's probably too late as they are married now but at least I feel I can still do something even if it's just protecting Mary's inheritance.'

'Yes, I've wondered about that myself. One day Mary will be a very wealthy lady.'

'That's what worries me.'

'I'm sorry but I can't promise anything David, otherwise just try and not worry too much, things generally have a way of working out and I'll keep Mary safe.'

Edward looked affectionately at his brother and wished he could have retired years ago though he knew in the back of his mind that Bella would somehow had put her foot down. He really didn't like her and would have liked David to have married someone else.

David had enjoyed his brother's company and wished he could see more of him. He trusted him and hoped he would be able to help. The wedding in some ways had been far too quick and David bitterly regretted being pushed into making quick decisions from his wife. He would have a word with George and was glad Jimmy might be able to help. Jimmy he thought, he'd always liked him, he'd become an Inspector and at such a young age. If only... he stopped himself, if only Jimmy was here to protect Mary, but from what, he thought to himself. From Albert Smithers he replied aloud.

Edward walked with David back to the station and when the train was out of sight, he bought a newspaper and sat by the platform reading the day's headlines. His mind kept going back to the conversation he'd just had with his brother. He was very fond of David and now that he was living in England, he felt closer to him. He scratched his head and felt slightly guilty.

What David hadn't seen was the look of concern on Edward's face. When David had telephoned him, Edward hadn't been entirely surprised by his concern about Albert Smithers. Being a solicitor, he had taken it upon himself and had made several enquiries and had so far ascertained that James Smithers had been meeting with his bank manager more frequently than needed of late and had recently set up several off shore accounts in the Cayman Islands. Of course there was nothing of too much concern in that alone but just last week he'd been privy to a conversation from one of his friends in the city who'd mentioned that there was a lot of activity in the capital saying that the Smithers 'family were more or less on the edge of bankruptcy.

Edward knew better than to listen to idle gossip but he also knew usually there was no smoke without fire and in this case like David the more he'd listened to gossip about Albert Smithers, the more he started to dislike him. In truth, David was right to mistrust Albert and his father James. They were it seems from all the talk, a family to avoid and now as far as Edward was concerned they had somehow become a relative albeit from marriage.

Edward had been busy all week with various important contracts at work and had been in and out of the office.

He'd been a senior partner for Thistle & Woods, in London for nearly two years. He enjoyed his work but more importantly loved his family. Verity his wife was English. They met whilst studying Law at Oxford. When the opportunity came for Edward to work in England, Verity was delighted. They settled in a large manor home in a country village outside the city. Soon after the move, the twins came along, George and Beatrice who were now nearing on three years.

Life for Edward was perfect and he wished things could have been the same for his brother. Still at least David had Mary who thankfully despite having been shown little affection as a child through an uncaring mother and busy father somehow had made a lovely young woman.

After several days, Edward had given the matter of Albert Smithers much thought but hadn't been able to see Jimmy. As the week went by however, luckily he found that he would after all be able to finish work early that Friday and so arranged to meet him for a couple of drinks after work at the Stag Pub by the side of the courts.

The Pub was a regular haunt for solicitors and generally attracted people of the law including police officers, it was positioned just off Whitehall, a stones throw away from Edward's offices. By now it was late afternoon and Edward sat at the far end of the pub, whilst looking for his friend. Although he'd not been able to visit England frequently, he'd known Jimmy as a young boy. He was pleased he'd become an Inspector. He was a pleasant type of chap who'd started his career as a beat bobby in Lambeth's East End. His easy going manner yet quick sharp mind soon meant that he risen up the ranks to be promoted.

He was a good looking man and had been courting a young girl. Just before an engagement was announced, sadly last year his lady friend, Ivy had died after a terrible fever had took hold of her. Jimmy had been devastated by her sudden death and even though about the same time, he'd been made Inspector, it had been a cruel blow. Edward had taken it upon himself to try and meet him for a couple of drinks every now and again but not as much as he'd have liked. Though Jimmy was younger than him, he enjoyed his company.

He liked listening to Jimmy's recollections of what his life was like as a boy at Herron Hall and the antics he and Mary used to get up to. Edward liked his niece and knew that Jimmy as a younger boy had been kind to her.

Jimmy's likeable manner allowed him to mix comfortably with both criminals and yet at the same time he also was able to rub shoulders with the top echelons of the law. He was a clever young man who was also very good at his job.

Edward too had been lucky enough to find out early in life that as a general rule if you happen to like someone enough, that's when you tell them things you're not supposed to. Following this example had made Jimmy an excellent detective.

'Well, well, if it's not old Edward,' Jimmy laughed and got up from his seat to welcome his friend. 'It's been a few months now, I think we both work too hard.'

'It's always nice to see you,' Edward replied as he shook Jimmy's hand. 'And less of the old please. I must say we're seeing busy times in the city at the moment.'

'Well, I'm not much of a business man myself, still if I was of a certain mind, I would have taken up with some of

65

the East End gangs a long time ago and sailed off to New York,' Jimmy said smiling.

'Well there's no time like the present to start. Mind there's only one way for shares to go and it won't be up,' Edward shook his head more to himself than to Jimmy.

Edward drank the rest of his pint thoughtfully. 'Anyway 1927 has been a good year so far, so let's toast to that,' Edward said as he raised his pint in jest.

'Here, here and no more talk of investments.'

Jimmy smiled and couldn't help but feel that Edward hadn't changed a bit. It had to be said that along with his brother, he was one of the cleverest people he knew.

Jimmy had loved his childhood living at Herron Hall. Although he knew David better, he'd enjoyed Edward's visits as he was nearer his own age than David. Both men had been very kind to him and had always treated his parents like family. Even Bella had tolerated him, though this could not be said for all her staff.

'Anyway,' continued Jimmy. 'The way Italy and Europe's going at the moment with Mussolini, who knows what will happen.'

'Testing times my friend,' Edward said. 'It's Germany we need to watch out for. '

'I believe so,' agreed Edward.

'Poverty always brings trouble, believe you me I should know that's what keeps me in a job,' Jimmy said smiling.

Both men laughed, totally at ease in each other's company.

'So, what's this business with Albert Smithers you mentioned on the phone?' Jimmy sipped his pint curious as to know what was on his Edward's mind. 'I must say I thought Mary looked beautiful for her wedding. She made a stunning bride. She sometimes writes but not as much since...Well since when I met Ivy and well... after Ivy's death. I guess it was difficult for her to write,' he said biting his lip.

'Yes I'm so sorry how things worked out,' Edward said.

'It's been a difficult few years... anyway,' Jimmy said wanting to change the subject. 'I must say Albert Smithers was a big surprise. My father was horrified. He told me he'd tried to warn David but in some ways it's not entirely his place.'

'It's a tricky business, I felt pretty much the same. I said as much as I could but…' Edward said. The courtship was very hasty, far too quick, I'd say.'

'Yes, that's more or less what everyone has thought, between you and me, I think it's been Bella who has pushed things,' Jimmy sighed.

'Most likely, I think she has always more or less gotten her own way.'

Edward hesitated.

He needed Jimmy's help but what was it he was asking for. A hunch that Albert was a bad man sounded absurd. Like himself Jimmy was a man of the law, who only dealt with facts, guessing was not how the law worked. Edward though wasn't asking for himself, he was asking for his brother and his niece Mary. There was also another reason for his reluctance to ask Jimmy too many questions. What if he were to uncover some information from his friend that he didn't want to know.

Sensibly, Edward knew that generally in life the more questions you asked then you may not want to know the answers and for his brother's sake maybe it was better he didn't know the truth. Still he decided to question Jimmy, if he didn't he may regret it.

'Well, to be quite frank, I think there's some funny business going on with Smithers,' Edward said trying to think factually. 'It makes me wonder that somehow Mary has got involved way over her head and has only married Albert just to please her parents,' he continued knowing this part of the story to be true.

'Well it's not a crime to marry for money, let's face it, women do it all the time so if a man does every now and again what's wrong with that?'

'That's true,' Edward said and laughed.

'Why, if I put a woman away every time she'd married for money, our jails would be full,' Jimmy laughed but knew his friend better than to poke fun of.

He knew Edward was not the sort of person that would cause a fuss or make accusations easily so whatever it was that had upset him, it had to be based on some truth.

'Look Edward, I've got some information but I can only say so much. Albert Smithers is not my usual clientele mind, but nonetheless.' Jimmy looked around making sure no one could hear. 'Smithers 'name was loosely linked with a case that I've been working on.'

'Confidential of course,' Edward said.

'Of course, confidentiality goes with the territory I'm afraid,' Jimmy smiled. 'Look Edward, I'll make some enquiries though if it's anything big, people aren't liable to talk too much, it's just the way it goes.'

'Come now Jimmy, I'm sure you have ways and means of making people talk,' Edward joked and was now laughing and Jimmy joined in.

'Not so much, especially as times are changing. Why, these big time Charlies can be truly nasty. There's been a big increase in organised crime around the east of the river but inevitably it soon appears in the nicer parts of the big cities especially here in London.'

Edward raised an eyebrow as he listened carefully to Jimmy.

'I wouldn't have Smithers down as being involved in anything so big as that?' Edward asked surprised where the conversation was leading. 'He's a dubious character but gangs and crime, well that's something else.'

'You can never say anything about anyone or anything, they teach you that on the force, it's the very first rule of being a detective,' Jimmy said looking at his friend. 'And I might add the last rule is that appearances can be deceptive.'

Edward scratched his head trying to make sense of what Jimmy had said. Jimmy was a plain spoken man and in his line of work he probably had to think the worst of people, even so if Smithers was involved in some sort of crime gangs, well that certainly put a different slant on things.

The twenties as a decade, had seen rapid changes in society especially after the war, the very fabric of people's beliefs and values were so different from the turn of the century. Some of the wealthy, had embraced new social cultures and flamboyance and money was at the forefront of people's minds.

'Look if Smithers is involved in anything too big, believe you me it will eventually all come out in the wash,' Jimmy said trying to reassure Edward.

'That's what bothers me.'

'Well in some ways it should,' said Jimmy sensibly.

'The thing is, Mary has married Smithers and my brother is bitterly regretting that decision. He's a clever man and sensibly most of his money is tied up at the moment in investments and not in Mary.'

'That's wise.'

'Well yes, but if anything were to happen to David then it's Mary who inherits most of the money,' Edward said thoughtfully. 'It's been a difficult decision for David to know what to do for the best.'

'At least your brother has shown sense, making sure Smithers doesn't immediately get his grubby hands on the entire estate but more's the pity he only had one child, having a son would have been a whole lot easier, ties things up more,' Jimmy remarked not liking the sound of the situation and seeing his friend's predicament.

'Still now Mary has come of age she is a very wealthy woman in her own right and of course as I have said she is the sole beneficiary of most of David's estate which is worth a hell of a lot of money I reckon my brother also has more businesses than both Bella and Mary know about.'

'Really,' Jimmy smiled in jest. He knew David had no dubious business dealings but he still liked the thought of teasing his friend.

'I'm afraid you're barking up the wrong tree,' Edward said wagging his finger. 'That brother of mine is perfectly legit of course. David's always been good in business and I'm guessing that he has a finger in every pie, here and there but I bet he's damned good at running them.'

'Money can be a real problem in families, if you ask me it causes most squabbles,' Jimmy replied. 'It really is the root of all evil.'

'You're right Jimmy, it's a tricky business. From a solicitors 'point of view, money can break up families in an instant.'

'I'm guessing Bella was a wealthy woman in her own right before marriage.' Jimmy remarked now picturing Bella in his mind. 'And I'm also guessing some of her money may have gone into some of those businesses.'

'But that's the strangest thing, you see in all these years from David knowing Bella, he has never once in conversation talked about her past.'

'Really, how strange.'

'Yes, it's as though he doesn't want to think about it. I'm just guessing but I get the impression that Bella's parents were extremely wealthy,' Edward said thoughtfully. 'Yet from what I can surmise, it would seem Bella has little money of her own.'

'What are you implying?'

'That somehow her parents chose not to leave any money to her.'

'You mean cut her out of any inheritance? '

'Exactly.'

'But why?' Jimmy said. 'There must have been reason, probably a big fall out.'

'It would explain things.'

'Maybe you've always been right not to trust Bella. I also think your brother is sensible to question Smithers ' motives.'

Jimmy sighed, he wanted to help. The truth was he wished things could have turned out differently. If truth be known he'd always had a soft spot for Mary. He knew however it was never to be. Mary was younger than him and from an early age, he'd wanted to get away from the Hall and pursue his career in London.

It was a gamble that had paid off but his plans had no place for Mary and life being life meant other things had got in the way. He'd been devastated by Ivy's death a couple of years ago. She was a lovely girl and he'd been awfully fond of her but it was Mary he carried a torch for.

Not that he thought, she knew his feelings or socially he could ever match the likes of Albert Smithers but nevertheless he could sense Mary felt the same about him. He knew deep down David like Bella had wanted a man for Mary that could match her wealth. Somehow though his gut instinct had also told him that David would have trusted him enough to know that he could perhaps have given Mary a life of love and security, traits that Albert never could. He also was wise enough to know Bella would have never felt the same as David and because of that, he consoled himself he wasn't meant to be with Mary.

Edward interrupted his thoughts. 'If Mary was my daughter I wouldn't like the situation but it will be difficult to point the finger at anything substantial.'

'Yes,' Jimmy went on. 'As detectives, we can always can get the bait but never the big fish. I'm afraid police budgets never stretch into the shady nets of deep waters.'

Edward appreciated Jimmy's time and didn't want to take any more of the conversation. Edward looked down at his watch.

'I'd better be going and I'm grateful for your advice.'

'Leave it with me Edward and I'll see if I can pull a few strings but I can't promise you anything.'

'I wouldn't expect it,' Edward replied.

Jimmy smiled and grabbed his wallet. 'By the way, remember me to Mary. Tell her to write. I'd still like to keep in touch.'

'Of course.'

The pub had started to get busy and Edward wanted to take the train home for a relatively early evening to be with his family.

After a few minutes of small talk, the two friends went their separate ways. Time had passed quickly and Edward hurried back to the station.

It was as he neared the platform that he was aware of a man who he'd previously noticed in the pub where he'd just been. There seemed nothing unusual in that but Edward sensed the man watching him, which made him feel suspicious.

It was a cold evening and the strong breeze seemed biting. Edward fastened his coat and stood in the small shelter on the platform. He looked around trying to catch a glimpse of the man but could no longer see him.

Rubbing his eyes, Edward thought that perhaps it was his imagination playing tricks. All this talk of Albert and James Smithers and the gangs of the East End had made him feel jittery.

Though the train was on time, it was very crowded but luckily Edward spotted a seat in the carriage at the front which looked less busy. He quickly sat down, removed his hat and after making himself comfortable, looked out of the window, glad to be going home.

That's when he noticed the same man's reflection in the glass. Edward turned round and the man was standing outside the carriage. Edward didn't think it was just a coincidence, he felt he had been followed, though the reason for this he was unsure about.

The man must have guessed his thoughts and had moved further down the train. Instinctively Edward got out of his seat to follow. He made his way down the busy train which was full of commuters. When he got to the end of the train, the man had completely vanished. Edward retraced his steps and returned to his seat. He looked around but the man was nowhere to be seen. He got out his newspaper and started to read, trying to busy his mind.

The journey always went quickly and as he neared his station he put his paper away in his briefcase.

He checked to see if the man was still there but couldn't see him. Edward got off the train ready to get a taxi to take him home. It was as he was getting in the taxi, that as he looked behind him, that's when he saw the same man. This time the man smiled at him. Rather foolishly, Edward got out of the taxi, to confront the man but he quickly walked away.

'Who are you, what business do you have?' Edward asked cautiously.

At first there was no reply.

'Stay away from Jimmy Roberts, if you know what's good for you, or you'll regret it.'

Suddenly Edward was confronted by a tall bulky man. He looked dishevelled, was unshaven and his cap had a hole in the front. He looked at Edward and laughed, showing a weathered face, etched with lines and creases, someone who'd seen rather too much of life.

'Why do you want me to stay away from Jimmy?' Edward asked, though unnerved, he needed to know what the threat was about.

'Just do it, or you and your family may soon find out. '

The man clenched his fist tightly. Edward noticed that he had a tattoo of a ship which ran all the way down his knuckles. Edward looked the man in the eye. This man meant business and Edward was in no situation to argue.

'My boss is not as understanding as myself, if you know what I mean?'

Edward hesitated unsure what to say. 'Yes, very much so.'

It was an honest answer though Edward's voice was not surprisingly slightly shaky. The taxi was still waiting by the platform and Edward knew it was time to go, the quicker he got away, the better. On the journey home, Edward allowed himself to think about the man he had just met. His warning had certainly scared him, surely this had to be connected to Albert Smithers. His head was spinning with ideas but for now he couldn't piece them together. Whatever it was Albert was hiding, Edward got the impression it was something his brother didn't want to find out about.

It occurred to him that Jimmy may know more than he was letting on. Edward reasoned that the man on the train was part of something bigger than he first thought. He wouldn't be intimidated but from now on, he needed to be careful to whom he spoke to.

By 7 o'clock Edward arrived back home. He'd had some time to reflect about Albert and realised that David's concerns were well founded. Time was what he needed and sometimes he thought that was the one thing that perhaps David as well as Mary may not have the luxury of having. Edward started to feel worried about his brother and niece and wondered how safe they really were. He tried to make the phone call to Jimmy but he wasn't answering. Giving way to exhaustion he went to bed with the promise he'd contact him in the morning.

# Chapter 9

About two weeks later, David sat down in his study. He still had doubts about Albert. David had heard no news from Edward and contemplated whether or not to telephone. David knew that he was almost as busy as himself and so he felt it better not to bother him working on the basis that if he had any news then he would tell him.

David thought back to the wedding as he watched his daughter walk down the aisle. At the time, his own mind was filled with uneasiness yet at the same time Mary had seemed happy, in reflection, it was as though she had already resigned herself to becoming Albert's wife.

Bella had been so preoccupied by the wedding and all the endless preparations that ran alongside it, that he hadn't had a chance to talk to her. He knew she'd been over the moon by the ceremony and had talked endlessly about how wonderful it had been and how lucky Mary was.

Predictably, Bella had got totally carried away by events and the wedding had cost David a small fortune not that he minded. Having completed all his paperwork for the day, he decided to go downstairs and into the front room, it was as he passed the library that he overheard someone on the telephone. As he listened, he realised it was Bella.

'It's too late, I'm not happy how things are going, the plans have changed. I never agreed to this,' Bella's voice seemed quieter than normal.

Alarmed, David tried to catch more of the conversation but Bella by now had put the receiver down. David felt puzzled as to who she was talking to, perhaps it was one of the charities that Bella was patron to. David was concerned and wondered who was on the other end of the line. Bella had always had her own life and long ago David accepted that but for a few months now, Bella hadn't quite been herself. He'd naturally put this down to the wedding but now that it was over he no longer could hide behind this. Bella was up to something but he knew better than to confront her so for now he would do nothing.

It didn't stop David feeling worried. Again, he was half tempted to phone Edward but didn't want to make any kind of fuss and besides he knew that his brother would probably be in court this time of afternoon so he decided against it.

Jimmy Roberts looked at his desk seeing nothing but a pile of mounting paper work which had never been his favourite part of the job. He'd soon realised early in his career that the more he had climbed the ranks of the constabulary, unfortunately the more paper work landed his way.

'Sir there's a telephone call, do you want to take the call or shall I take a message,' the clerk said.

More out of boredom Jimmy decided to take the call, anything seemed better than the monotony of dealing with paper work.

'Yes, put them through Jessie.'

Jimmy balanced the hand receiver, pushing his pen top up and down, it was a habit he'd always had when concentrating and often annoyed his fellow workers.

'Hello, Chief Inspector Roberts, can I help you at all? ' he asked casually thinking what he was going to eat for lunch.

'It's Jude, Chief Inspector you know last week you asked me about Albert Smithers.'

'Yes.'

'Well there's been some information,' said a gruff sounding voice on the other end of the line. 'It'll cost you minds but the more information, the higher the price.'

'What exactly am I paying for?' Jimmy said trying to sound nonchalant, as in truth the telephone call had taken him somewhat by surprise.

'I've found something out but it's not the kind of thing someone like me tells on a phone line, we need to meet,' Jude said sharply sounding impatient. 'Busy man I am.'

Jimmy hesitated, the more he put this paper work off, the more he knew it would keep growing and it needed to be completed by the month's end which was getting closer by the day. Still he was very concerned about Edward and David. Jude was good at being a snitch, he mixed in the right circles. He'd helped him a few months back with a case he'd been working on which amounted to several arrests. He needed Jude as much as he didn't want to admit it, now he was worried for his niece Mary, he cleared his throat and went on.

'Well, I'm pretty tied up here,' Jimmy answered honestly taking the last mouthfuls of some cold tea left on his desk. 'So if you've got something, it'd better be good.'

'Well, it just so happens I'm down at Iron's Road tomorrow about three, I'll catch you near the bridge on the left side, right at the bottom.'

The line went quiet as Jimmy considered this proposal very carefully, his detective mind was suddenly switched on. He knew Jude was on to something. The old adage you get what you pay for however applied to Jude and his information never came cheap. Jimmy knew he'd want a favour or two in return but he thought he could negotiate the finer details later.

'Alright, I'll see you about three but it might be a little later as I'm coming across the city.'

'I'll wait.'

'Stay there until about half past and after that, take it I got tied down here,' Jimmy reasoned, his heart racing a little. Perhaps Jude would have some real dirt on Albert.

'Three o'clock then.'

'Three it is.'

Jimmy put the phone down and wondered if he should let Edward know about his meeting but he decided not for two reasons, firstly Jude might not come up trumps with any information at all and secondly, he might tell him some news that perhaps Edward was better off not knowing. The old expression, ask no questions tell no lies, came into Jimmy's mind.

London generally by late afternoon in the East End was shrouded in smog. The factories had all but come late last century just before Victoria's reign had come to an end. The twenties were now a result of a country whose industrial revolution had forever changed the fabric of Britain. The factories were here to stay and with it was the smog and the thick fogs that came in from the estuary of the Thames.

Iron's Road was not unlike any road around the east of the river. It ran parallel to the water and was set aside from the main factories. The road itself was adjacent to some derelict waste ground that had already been earmarked by a shipping company to build another factory. Rumour was that the owner had already started work unofficially as he already owned a fair amount of the docks. Bit by bit the landscape was changing and as a result all the problems that came with change were as well.

The other half of the street had small back to back houses that had been built a few decades earlier but as different tenants moved in and out, of late the houses had started to look derelict and run down. Jimmy knew any area that looked like this quickly gave rise to crime, first came petty thieving but in recent years a notorious gang had swept through the area.

Debt collectors frequented the streets and there was a forever growing atmosphere of fear and tension which played into the gangs' hands. Dominic Rocco virtually owned every road from as far as Sydney Street to a mile or so down the Thames. He had been born from Italian immigrants and from his teens formed a gang who had gone on to terrorise the neighbourhood. From his meteoric rise to power, it meant that he now ruled with an iron fist and over the years through his vile bullying, racketeering and extortion, it had made him a very wealthy man. He now lived in Sloane Square, a million miles from the sweat grime and tears of the area.

Jimmy made good time as he walked along the bridge that ran into Iron's Road and was pleased to see his watch read just past three. He looked up and down the street but there was no sign of Jude. He was usually on time but perhaps he'd been out running an errand for someone, probably Rocco.

It had turned cold so he put his hands in his pocket to tighten his coat.

A few minutes had passed but still there was no sign of Jude. The noise of the street was deafening and he could hear the machinery working at full pace from the factories behind where thick black puffs of smoke bellowed out in quick succession.

After several more minutes, he was just about to head back to his car when he heard the distinct click of a gun behind him. He slowly turned and found a man about in his mid thirties, pointing the barrel of a gun straight in his face. 'One move and you're for it,' the man said in a deep sounding voice. 'Any weapons lay them on the ground. Nice and slowly does it.'

Jimmy glanced around, there was no sign of Jude. A horrible thought struck him, one that seemed obvious now. Somehow he'd been set up and yet he could hardly believe it. Jude sailed very close to the wind but he was no real criminal, something was wrong.

'Alright,' Jimmy said. 'Easy does it.'

He needed time to think, and was desperately trying to buy a few seconds to formulate a plan. 'Let me get my gun from my pocket, what's this all about, where is Jude?'

'Let's just say you won't be hearing from your little snitch for a long, long time.'

'What did you do with him?' Jimmy asked but he already knew the answer, people like this came only to kill.

'Too many questions from you and we don't want anyone getting any answers do we now,' the man said and Jimmy noticed a large scar that ran across his right cheek.

His clothes gave no indication where he was from nor did his accent but Jimmy knew it was not from around this part of London.

'I just wanted to know.'

'You guessed it, he's dead, my boss doesn't need little tittle tattlers like that, too nosy for their own good, that's what I say, too damned nosy.'

Jimmy was quiet, he didn't scare easily and looked more closely at the man. He was tall with a stocky build. His hair was greying at the sides and apart from the scar on his face, there were no unusual features that made him stand out. He'd more or less fit the description of half the men Jimmy had put behind bars over the years.

'Smithers, did he put you up to this?' Jimmy was playing for time and wanted answers fast.

'I said no questions but I'll tell you what, I'm feeling generous Detective Roberts today, if you must know, yes, a very big trader let's just say in women's jewellery, in fact I'll make it very easy, it's the sort that sparkles.'

'Diamonds,' Jimmy said.

'You heard me.'

Jimmy could have never have guessed that's what this was all about, smuggling diamonds into the country. He'd heard that a shipment of diamonds just last week had been found from a vessel that was registered to Johannesburg but had had its documents falsified to say it was from Cadiz in Spain. Customs were apparently tearing their hair out about this and here he was about to be shot at point blank as a result from a tip off from a grass that was already dead. His friend's brother had just married his daughter into what could only be described as a cartel of diamond smugglers. It almost made him laugh, the force had certainly taught him that in life, the strangest things happened.

'Well, aren't we clever Chief Inspector and for that... '

The man hit the trigger but as he did so Jimmy pulled his other gun that was hooked in his sleeve and shot. He never missed and even now although his main job was sitting in an office, in training he still scored perfect tens. The shot went right through the man's heart. He staggered back, dazed and perhaps it was a lapse in judgement on Jimmy's part but the man pulled the trigger of his gun, and as if by his dying wish he suddenly raised his arm high in the air and shot Jimmy just missing his heart by millimetres.

The shot was enough to knock Jimmy off his feet and blood quickly started pouring from his chest. He knew in a few minutes if he did nothing, he would be dead. He needed help and needed it straight away.

His car was parked too far away back near the bridge and he knew that he would never make it there. He was fighting for his life and he had to think fast before he passed out. With literally only seconds left to spare, he remembered his whistle that he still kept in his jacket pocket and with his last few breaths of consciousness, he blew it as hard and loud as he could. It must have been a stroke of luck because in the nearby factories the workers' shift changed at four on the dot.

The men would have worked an eight hour shift starting early at seven in the morning having stopped for lunch and then gone onto work a four hour long haul in the afternoon. The night workers by half past three were starting to come in from nearby areas ready to change into their overalls and clock in. Two men in the outer lobby had just arrived and were just about to register for their shift when they heard gun shots and guessed the noise was coming from Iron's Road. They didn't quite know what to think at first and then when they heard the whistle this confirmed that somebody was in trouble. Two big burly men started to run from the factory towards the river. The taller of the two was a little more wary as they got towards the bridge.

They'd been some trouble just a few nights ago from two rival gangs and he didn't want to get too involved in anything that they couldn't handle. He stopped them both as they got to the foot of the river.

'Careful, keep a look out.'

'Quick Pete, duck down, I think I can see two men, as far as I can tell, they're lying on the ground and it looks like they've been shot.'

'How?' Pete said who was regretting leaving the factory where they were safe of any danger.

'I'm not sure what's happened but check to see if there's no one else around,' said Bill who was a lot younger than Pete and started quickly scouring the area.

'Will do.'

'Keep low but my guess is they've scarpered off whoever they are.'

Bill was concerned but knew they should still go and see if they could be of any help.

'Ay,' Pete answered more unsure of what to make of the situation than his friend.

Both men ran quickly to the embankment and could clearly see a man lying on the floor, he looked like he'd sustained terrible injuries. Suddenly Pete noticed a second man who was also lying on the grass by the side of the river and looked as if he'd been shot as well.

'Blimey it's only Jimmy Roberts, he's now an Inspector,' Pete said in disbelief.

'How do you know?' Bill asked trying to make sense of what had happened.

'Because, he banged my brother in law away for five years on robbery charges last March. Like a Jack Russell gnawing away he is, got his just deserve I say.'

'That's a bit harsh after all the man was only doing his job.'

'Look, this is way over our heads, let's just get out of here, I say we leave both of them, Jimmy Roberts looks as dead as a door nail by the looks of it and we don't want things to get messy.'

Pete was already turning around and starting to walk away.

'What about Roberts though we can't just go and leave him here?' Bill asked not liking the thought of leaving the two bodies and especially if Roberts was still alive. If somebody had seen them near the scene, then they might be implicated in something they didn't want to be.

'Leave him.'

'No, wait,' Bill looked carefully at Jimmy. Quick Pete, he's still breathing you can't just leave him, I won't let you, we have to try and save him,' Bill said his conscience now getting the better of him.

Bill was ten years younger than Pete which made him less cynical of life and although the thought of helping the law didn't sit easy with him neither did leaving a man to die either. Besides if anyone had seen them it might make the situation worse.

'We don't want to make it worse. Pete, if we've been seen here and leave this mess, you've just signed our death warrant. They'll hang us for him.'

'You're kidding,' Pete said thinking that to help now seemed the better idea.

'Pete, you go back to work, we don't need to tell the lads at the factory but meanwhile I'd better do a detour onto Northumberland Street, there's a local police station on there. Mind, looking at this little mess, the police are going to want to investigate this properly. It looks to me as though this man tried to shoot Jimmy and he shot him first but for Roberts, maybe it's too late.'

'Do you think he'll live?' Pete asked.

'It's hard to say, I'll go now and get help, mind I think more questions will be asked, this case is bigger than the local police station, they'll send the big guns in from the Met,' Bill said still checking that no one had seen them or was watching from a distance.

'What do you think it's all about?' Pete asked now intrigued by how Jimmy Roberts had ended up half dead in a run down area in the East End.

'What most crime is all about, you should know that by now, it's all about money, good old fashioned money, the stuff that makes the world go round. It can build a man up with great fortunes and then bring him crashing down.'

'Thought that was love,' Pete laughed trying to relieve the situation but inside he desperately wanted to get away and go back to the factory, in case more trouble followed. After all he thought to himself, if there was one gang in the neighbourhood then it was highly likely there could be other members lurking around.

'Well if you believe love is more important than money then you're a bigger fool than I had you down for,' said Bill and chuckled to himself.

# Chapter 10

Le Touquet for those that have had the pleasure to visit, is a beautiful small seaside town in northern France and the 1920's had cemented it to be one of the chicest places to visit in Europe. The large hippodrome had been recently built on the sea front with no expense spared and housed the many plays where budding artists and amateur thespians could have the opportunity to tread the boards of the theatre and show off their talents in front of a captive audience from the wealthiest parts of Europe.

Mary and Albert had chosen Le Grand Hotel which was situated on the sea front. It was very impressive and despite having been built in the 1850's it still remained at the forefront of fashion. Numerous famous people from aristocracy, actors and top military over the years had visited and the guest book was certainly one to boast.

Mary had chosen a suite that had a fantastic view overlooking the seafront and the room had every comfort they could wish for. Four tennis courts were situated at the side of the hotel and there was an outdoor sea pool which was very popular amongst guests. Although the hotel was always busy, the management made sure that all guests were made to feel special. It was truly luxurious and Mary was very pleased with her choice.

Luckily the weather had been very warm of late and Mary was enjoying playing tennis, swimming and walking and relaxing in the hotel's extensive grounds. The entertainment was extremely popular and the evenings often centred around the grand piano in the large hall and various singers both French and English each night, wooed their audience with the most magnificent singing filling the main hall.

Albert had been pleasant company and Mary had enjoyed the first few days of her honeymoon but by the

Wednesday of the first week, Albert was back to his usual distracted self.

'Mary, there's somebody I have to see, he lives in Paris and is playing golf here in Le Touquet this afternoon,' Albert said giving no indication as to whom he was meeting.

'You're kidding Albert, it's our honeymoon and I'd planned to play croquet at three. There's a small group of us and after we were going to have a few drinks on the terrace,' Mary answered trying not to sound disappointed.

'Honey, you're being unreasonable.'

'I don't think so but if that's what you have to do then so be it,' Mary said. 'Besides I can soon busy myself.'

'You know I love you.'

Since being married, Albert seemed to be trying hard to change his manner. Mary though knew better than to read anything into it other than the fact that Albert was trying too hard and pretending to be someone he wasn't.

The word pretend, had started to echo in Mary's mind of late and she got the feeling that there was a side of Albert that she really didn't know and he had managed so far to keep well hidden. It made her feel wary and on her guard which she thought wasn't such a bad thing after all.

'Look Mary, there's some lovely boutiques on the sea front, here buy a few dresses and treat yourself and I'll see you tonight,' Albert said impatiently as though he wanted to get somewhere fast.

With that, Albert threw some crumpled notes on the bed and quickly went through the large wooden door that led into the central hall. Mary looked down at the money, it wasn't even enough to buy one dress let alone several but feeling frustrated and let down by Albert's behaviour, she decided nevertheless to venture into the small seaside town.

Mary spoke French moderately well so decided to ask if there were any new stage acts performing at the Hippodrome. She hadn't seen a play for a while and the thought of taking in a few shows one evening would make a pleasant change.

Dressed in a casual linen dress and straw bag with her petite slim frame, Mary herself could have easily been mistaken for a local French woman. She soon realised that the shops she wanted were located slightly behind the beach which seemed to stretch endlessly for miles. She favoured one particular dress which was far more than the money Albert had given her but with a little added from her purse after an hour or so, she came out of the shop happy with her purchases.

It was really hot by now and as it was still early afternoon, she decided to keep walking around the narrow cobbled streets. She purposely walked down the alleyways which were sheltered giving herself a welcome break from the heat of the sun. Mary was enjoying her stroll and could only admire the quaintness of the resort. Her attention however was suddenly drawn to the little apartments above the shops which were painted in bright blue almost matching the colour of the sky.

Mary became aware of voices which seemed to be coming from the next street around the corner. Mary instantly recognised one of the voices straight away, it was unmistakable, as it was Albert's and the other voice was definitely a woman's. Not wanting to be seen, she instinctively ducked beneath one of the canopies which overhung a cafe so she couldn't be spotted.

The voices were not getting any louder or further which suggested they were probably sitting in one of the cafes which lined the front. Curiosity getting the better of her, she slowly edged forward not wanting to be seen yet desperate to see who the female voice belonged to. She stood on her tiptoes and peered over a small fence filled with geraniums.

Although she knew the voice belonged to Albert, she was still shocked to see Albert sitting comfortably at a small table smoking alongside another woman. A waiter had now come into view and the couple were still discussing the menu wondering which wine to choose. Much to Mary's disappointment the angle at which the woman was sitting meant that Mary couldn't see the woman's face.

Mary wriggled backwards and forwards but as much as she tried, it was useless unless she stepped forwards and risked being seen and she therefore was unable to get a clear view. Five minutes or more must have passed by now and Mary knew she couldn't stay there as she sooner or later as she would draw suspicion.

The evening waiter at their hotel had warned them just last night, that there had been a rise in thefts recently in the resort, mainly from men arriving from the south of France and travelling north, aiming at the wealthy visitors who they regarded as easy prey.

Any longer snooping around, if Mary wasn't careful she might be accused of something she hadn't done but she was determined to try and see the woman. In a last attempt, Mary squeezed herself as near to the iron fence as she possibly could and that's when she could finally see the woman who was now laughing and being intimate with Albert.

As Mary looked again, it dawned on her that the woman's hair was auburn. This couldn't surely be a coincidence, this was now the third time that Mary had seen the woman over a few months, the first time was from her visit to Albert's home, Sewter Lodge. The next time was in the church at her wedding and now the same woman was here in Le Touquet, eating late lunch with Albert who was now her husband.

Mary kept asking herself over and over who this woman could be and more importantly what relevance she had to Albert. Maybe she should confront him and ask directly as she was now starting to suspect that the woman was Albert's lover. It didn't surprise her, Albert was not trustworthy, she'd known that from the start. She couldn't however stop feeling foolish. She'd imagined just for the sake of discretion he wouldn't be up to his antics quite as quickly.

Mary took a deep breath feeling anger rising in her. She needed to consider her position carefully, it wouldn't do to cause a scene with Albert here or in the hotel, after all it was her honeymoon and she must think of her own and her father's reputation. If word got out of any scandal then people would no doubt talk which would cause embarrassment to everyone.

No, she knew she must bide her time and wait patiently. If this woman was Albert's lover then at least she now knew. Mary was almost relieved that she knew of such things so early into the marriage. If truth be known she'd been expecting this, she'd often seen Albert's roving eyes around a pretty woman.

Her father had always taught her from being a little girl that it was better to be forewarned about a situation no matter how bad, it was better to know now rather than later. Now she could carefully steer the situation rather than await for a nasty awkward surprise later.

Though she was trying to think practically, she still felt upset and humiliated, by marrying a man like Albert, in truth it was almost to be expected. Still Albert had certainly not wasted any time after all she thought to herself, she'd not thought he'd be carrying on when they were still on their honeymoon.

Mary quickened her pace trying not to be too upset. She retraced her steps and returned to her room still having some time to herself. She knew she must act as though nothing had happened and more importantly give nothing away. If her behaviour suddenly changed, Albert may suspect something was wrong and for now, she knew something that he didn't want her to.

Mary also reminded herself that she still had a whole week of her honeymoon left but this could be to her benefit as it allowed her to sit and think and with that she put on her new dress, twisted her hair and suddenly tennis and croquet didn't seem that important. The hotel was divine, the weather wonderful and a week in France was still a luxury that despite everything she was determined to make the most of.

She deeply regretted marrying Albert but for now she knew would just have to accept her situation though it didn't make it any easier. She was beginning to dislike Albert Smithers more and more.

# Chapter 11

The weather in London had been abysmal for a few days now, it had rained all day long making it incredibly foggy. Edward enjoyed being a solicitor and was used to the ways of the law after all it was his job but he felt frustrated as he sat at Harrow Police Station.

The station was built around fifty years ago and looked as though no care had ever been taken. It was dilapidated and badly needed a fresh coat of paint. The paint on the walls had flaked and the windows rattled breaking the silence of the room. The phone call had taken Edward by surprise even more so when he was asked if he wouldn't mind coming down to the station for questioning about a friend of his.

When he had asked which friend, the man at the other end of the line had told him he'd rather discuss the matter at the station. After however being here for the best part of an hour with only a strong cold cup of coffee to show for it, his patience was more than a little tested. Suddenly the door opened and a rather rotund looking man probably in his late forties entered the room. He was balding and used his thinning hair on one side to drape across to the other. He looked at Edward in a suspicious manner which Edward dismissed as he'd never met an Inspector yet that didn't view everyone other than a suspect.

'Hello, I'm Detective Superintendent Howarth, sorry about dragging you to the station, all this I bet is most inconvenient.'

He shook Edward's hand and sat with a wedge of papers at the other side of his desk.

'Well what's this all about?' Edward sat back in his chair, if Howarth wanted to intimidate him then he would be mistaken. Although Howarth thought he was smart

Edward knew within a few seconds of meeting him that he was far smarter.

'Friend of Jimmy's, aren't you?'

'Well, yes, good friend I'd say but I've not seen him for a while, we're like that, I might not see him for weeks, we're both busy and then sometimes we bump into each other mostly in various London pubs,' Edward said and smiled at Howarth but felt he was being tested. 'What's Jimmy up to then as I've said I've not seen him for a while now?'

'You won't have,' Howarth said. 'He was on some police business and was shot a few days ago. We've only just this afternoon informed his next of kin. It could have gone either way but thankfully he became conscious a few days ago.'

Edward couldn't believe it, he thought back to the last time he'd seen Jimmy. That's when it dawned on him that somehow this might have something to do with Smithers, after all, he'd asked Jimmy to do some digging around.

He also remembered his journey home after meeting Jimmy, there had been the encounter with the man who had followed him on his train journey home and the threat he'd made to him to stay away from Jimmy. Edward couldn't bear to think that perhaps he'd rumbled onto something that he shouldn't have and that it could have been the trigger for the attempt on Jimmy's life.

Suddenly he felt that he was involved in something far bigger than he first thought. When he'd asked Jimmy for help, he'd no idea what he was unravelling and now he was seriously injured.

'How bad is he?' Edward asked sounding tense.

'Well, he's over the worst and thankfully because he's still young and healthy, I think he's going to pull through.'

'That's a relief, thank goodness for that,' Edward said still coming to terms with what he'd just heard.

'They removed the bullet from his chest and he's hoping to be released from hospital by next week.'

'That's great news, a lucky escape, I'd say,' Edward said with relief.

'When I spoke to him, he's hoping to go back to Herron Hall to be with his parents, George and Charlotte.'

'He'll be well looked after, he's like family.'

'I think it's fair to say, he'll be weak for a while,' Howarth said lighting a cigar which sent a strong aroma around the room. 'Right down to business, I bet you're wondering why you're here?

Howarth's manner was abrupt but again it didn't in anyway intimidate Edward.

'Yes, I am wondering what this has to do with me.'

'Well, although at the moment Jimmy is very weak, when I interviewed him, he told me a rather interesting story.'

'Yes.'

'About a man called Albert Smithers. The Smithers ' family aren't exactly new to us. They've been involved in criminal activity for a few years now.' Howarth paused reaching for his cup of tea. 'The only problem with most of these so called criminals is bloody catching them. You see without any real evidence, we've got nothing substantial to pin any crime on them.'

'I see,' Edward said sounding alarmed by the news. 'I'd no idea about any of this. I'm sure my brother knows nothing at all.'

'These people always cover their tracks. It makes life very difficult for us. But every now and again they get clumsy and that's when we catch them.'

Howarth paused looking at Edward then carried on. 'It would seem from different sources that the Smithers ' family are tied up in various unscrupulous money making schemes, some perhaps in the big league but that's the thing with criminal activity it breeds like wildfire.'

'I can't believe it,' Edward said abruptly. 'You're not suggesting for one minute that my brother is tied up in any of this?'

'No, nothing of the kind,' Howarth said reassuringly. 'I have it on good authority that David Green is as clean as a whistle. Keen business man but even paying his tax bills, it would seem is accountable.'

Edward felt insulted that his brother's name should be tarnished with the likes of James and Albert Smithers but he knew the police had to look at every possibility. It seemed just bad luck that Mary had married Albert. Edward could see only problems ahead.

The attack on Jimmy and the news of the Smithers was a lot for Edward to take in. Edward looked around the interview room which was very small and he was beginning to feel claustrophobic. He thought about Jimmy and hoped that he would soon be able to get back on his feet.

'Is Jimmy alright now?' Edward asked his mind racing for information.

'It's hard to say but it appears likely, he lost a lot of blood though. It seems that he owes his life to two factory workers who were swapping shifts and heard a whistle from Jimmy which alerted them.

They found him lying on Iron's Road in the East End. As I've said, luckily for him the bullet missed all his vital organs. The two factory men have been made heroes out of this whole damned thing,' Detective Howarth explained and looked quizzically at Edward.

'I guess he owes his life to them,' Edward said.

'Jimmy mentioned to me that he'd met you and you were worried about Albert.'

'Yes, we met a few weeks ago. It's David, he's worried about the family.'

'He should be,' Howarth said.

He wasn't a man to mince his words. Howarth looked at the clock, he needed to be somewhere and by now he'd gathered that Edward didn't know much about the attack on Jimmy.

'I might as well add at this stage if can you shed some light as to what happened to Jimmy,' Howarth asked. 'Sorry to put you in a quandary but nevertheless attempted murder is something we take seriously especially to one of our own.

This is very serious indeed though I'm sure I don't need to stress that point to someone such as yourself?'

Edward was a considered man so thought carefully before he spoke. 'Not really, though there is just one small thing I think I ought to mention, the evening I met Jimmy to tell him about the Smithers.'

'Yes, carry on.'

'Well... when I arrived at the station to catch my train, I noticed I was being followed,' Edward said and looked at Howarth to see his reaction. 'I thought it was my mind playing tricks, the man then got on the same train and got off at my station. I tried to talk to the man but he quickly scarpered off but not before he'd threatened me and told me to stay right away from Jimmy.'

'I see, this puts things in a different light,' Howarth said.

'I'm still not sure but it could be related to what's happened to Jimmy?' Edward suggested.

'Well, it was certainly a warning, but at this stage it's difficult to prove that either James or Albert are incriminated somehow in this. By the way Mr. Green, why did your brother agree to the union of his daughter and Albert?'

Edward answered thoughtfully. 'That's a good question, I was very surprised by the pairing but reading between the lines, I'd say it had more to do with his wife, Bella Green. David had doubts but once Mary said yes, as you can imagine, it's quite difficult to weave your way out of such things. Anyway the wedding still went ahead last week.'

'Right and where are Mary and Albert now?'

'They're on their honeymoon, Le Touquet in northern France.' Edward hesitated as he spoke. 'I've got to be honest with you, I feel guilty about Jimmy, you see it was me that asked him to do a bit of detective work.'

'I see and what exactly do you mean?'

'Well it was me that asked him to ask a few questions about Albert but I'd no idea that he would end up nearly dead, how could I?' Edward reasoned more with himself.

Edward looked at the Detective Howarth who seemed unlike most men of his age who are only too happy to just see in retirement, he however had still got the bit between his teeth and Edward could see he had been and still was a mighty fine police officer.

'It goes with territory, Jimmy knew what he was doing, the whistle was a clever idea and that's probably why he's still alive, in my opinion, most officers in that situation would have ended up dead.'

That much was true, as long as Edward had known Jimmy, he knew he didn't cower away from danger.

'Look, thank you Mr. Green for coming into the station, it's a bit nearer for you than Scotland Yard and once again I apologise for your wait but if there's anything else you can think of or hear, then here's a letterhead with my telephone number on. Just call it and Jenny my secretary will let me know.'

Edward took the piece of paper and put it in his coat pocket.

Howarth shook his hand. 'By the way if you should decide you want to visit him, he's at Kings Cross, just say my name and security will let you through.'

'I will. I've known Jimmy from being a young boy. His parents work for my brother. George has been a good friend to David over the years and we all think a lot of Jimmy. Mary will be upset, that I'm sure of.'

'I'm sorry things have taken a nasty turn,' Howarth said.

Edward stood at the door after shaking Howarth's hand. Edward had to ask the question before leaving. 'Do you think whoever's done this will still come after him?'

'Not if I have anything I do with it. Jimmy is also my friend but anyone who shoots at an officer on my watch, let's just say, the big guy at the top won't be shooting again.'

# Chapter 12

Edward's home was a large Manor Lodge in the heart of the Sussex countryside. He commuted to London in the week, often working long hours but weekends he kept to himself for his family.

The neat lawned garden at the front of the house was kept immaculate and over the years, an abundance of rose bushes had grown creating an array of colour and scent which was particularly potent in the summer months.

Edward sat at the back of the house on his terrace sipping a small brandy. He wore a troubled expression on his face. The news of Jimmy had shaken him to the core. He'd not contacted David yet only having heard the news earlier.

This whole business was getting out of hand. Poor Mary what had they done to her. He knew David was besides himself and with good reason. He thought of his recent visit to Herron Hall for Mary's wedding. Since then, he'd only seen his brother a few weeks ago when they'd met in Leeds. At the time Edward has been struck by how worried and gaunt David looked.

David has been so busy during the wedding and its preparations that he'd not been able to talk to his brother; there simply had been no opportunity without other guests being around.

There could be no doubt however that Mary's wedding had been a truly spectacular event and yet Edward felt no joy and knew like David there was trouble ahead. David had been in his thoughts for a few weeks now and Edward reasoned that this was for a good reason. He was just thinking how to tell David about Jimmy when thankfully the phone rang.

'Edward it's your brother on the phone,' Verity said.

'I'll take it in the library,' Edward said wondering how to broach the subject.

'Edward, I've just heard the news from George, it's Jimmy, someone's tried to kill him,' David said sounding hoarse.

'I know I've just come from the police station. It's a situation that I think we're all tied up in. David, do you think this is Albert and James' doing?'

'I'm not sure. I really can't say. The main thing is Jimmy's going to be alright. Thank God. George told me two factory workers saved his life. Fingers crossed he should make a speedy recovery. He's lucky in that he's got youth on his side. I can't believe this has happened. It's quite shocking. If Albert and James are involved then we both need to be careful. Next time one of us may not be so lucky.'

'I know I've also been threatened. '

'When?'

'A few weeks ago, they told me to stay away from Jimmy and now look what has happened?'

'You need to tell the police Ed.'

'I already have. A superintendent Howarth is in charge of the case.'

'That name seems to ring a bell but I can't remember why,' David remarked more to himself than Edward. 'It's sad to say but things could have been a lot worse. Jimmy could be dead,' David pointed out.

'Yes, it's a damned awful business. The thing is David... I feel a little responsible.'

'How can that be?'

'As you know, I asked Jimmy to find some information about either Albert or James,' Edward said. 'Now I'm perhaps putting two and two together but surely this has got something to do with both of them?'

David paused before speaking. 'I must say, I don't like it Ed, but what can we do?'

'By the way, does Mary know about Jimmy, you know she was awfully fond of him. She's sure to be upset?'

'No, she's not been told, she'll be home in two days. I'll be so glad when I can see her,' David said his voice sounding tense. 'Thankfully Jimmy is out of the woods, when he's feeling a bit better, he can keep an eye on Mary for me.'

'Maybe she'll be looking after him,' Edward laughed. 'By the way, how's the honeymoon gone?'

'I believe as well as can be expected. Bella still seems just as enthusiastic about the whole dammed thing.'

By now time was getting on and Edward could hear Verity his wife calling him for evening dinner.

'Look David I've got to go but just watch your back. By the way, I'm planning on coming to stay with you for a few days. I don't think Verity and the twins will come this time but it will be good for us to catch up.'

'Yes, it will be nice to see you,' David said feeling relieved knowing his brother would be visiting.

'I was just thinking about the wedding. It was a lovely day, the twins are too young to appreciate it but Verity said Mary looked stunning,' Edward said trying his best to cheer his brother.

'Yes, the wedding went really well, it's just this business with the Smithers, anyway keep in touch and Edward just keep your ears to the ground.'

'I know,' said Edward. 'You'll make a detective out of me yet.'

'You'd be a perfect candidate.'

# Chapter 13

With the recent warm weather Herron Hall had been busier than ever. The wedding had been the biggest event the house had seen in recent times. Slowly though, things were now getting back to normal much to David's relief.

A constant stream of staff kept coming and going from the house which was tiring and unsettling for David. Admittedly, he would be glad when Mary would be back from Le Touquet.

Making the most of the warm day, David thought he'd tend to his garden. Staff were employed to keep the vast gardens neat and in order but he allowed himself a small walled garden which ran alongside a part of the house.

Over the years various herbs and special plants grew in abundance. A large hedge had been planted which served to cut the chilling east winds from the North Sea. Here close to nature, David felt truly at home.

As it was a particularly warm afternoon, David spent a few hours pruning the rose heads and carefully put the clippers away in his garden box which reminded him to ask George to replace some broken glass from a nearby greenhouse.

George had been on David's mind of late. He had been very upset for George and his wife Charlotte. The shocking news that Jimmy their son had been shot had taken him by surprise. The incident had been very serious and Jimmy had been very lucky to still be alive.

David was pleased that Jimmy had chosen to stay with his parents back at the Hall for a few weeks to recover.

Feeling rather thirsty, he went back inside the house stopping first in the kitchens. David was a sociable man who thought nothing of taking lunch with Betty and the kitchen staff whom he regarded as family. Betty had been a member of staff before David bought the Hall and David valued her experience and loyalty.

'Any word on Jimmy?' David asked as he passed the large kitchen table where food was prepared.

'Yes, it's good news. Charlotte told me that he's nearly up to his old self,' Betty said smiling. 'It'll do him the world of good to be back here in fact Charlotte mentioned just this morning how much she is looking forward to him being back home.'

'Thank goodness he's going to be alright,' David said.

'A real lucky escape if you ask me. Mind I know he's done well becoming an Inspector but it's still a dangerous line of work,' Betty said practically. 'Will you now be working in your study?'

'Yes Betty, I'm afraid I've got lots of paper work to catch up on. I've not been as organised of late as I usually am.'

'Right you are, I'll be bringing you a drink. I'll up be in a few minutes,' Betty said as she got a glass from the cupboard. 'By the way, I'm just going down to the village. Will you be wanting anything?'

David smiled, Betty was always so kind. He was lucky to have inherited her when he purchased the Hall. She had also been pleased to stay on especially working for David. David always said she was the best treasure they had in the house.

'Thanks Betty, I think for now, I'm alright.'

'As you like.' Betty sighed looking hot and tired. 'I'll be glad when things finally get back to normal, not that the wedding wasn't nice but it was lots of hard work especially for yourself.'

'Yes, but it was great to put the hard work in for Mary though I'm afraid I'm not getting any younger,' David said and laughed.

'None of us are,' Betty said grinning. 'Well, I'll be getting on with things.'

So far Betty's day had been busy keeping her usual high standards and order in the kitchens. On Tuesday afternoons however, it just so happened that she had a few hours where she had some free time. Although officially she was off duty, she would sometimes run errands for Bella.

Making the most of the sunshine, she decided she'd walk through the Hall's grounds which led to the local village. Remembering David's drink, she went up the main staircase and down the corridor to the study. As the door was closed, she placed the tray with the lemonade he'd asked for on a nearby table. She knocked on the study door aware that David often made lengthy telephone calls.

Being aware time was getting on, Betty knocked again this time more loudly. There was still no answer which was not entirely unusual. Betty's courteous nature meant that she simply left the tray on the table, then speaking loudly so David could hear through the door, she told him his drink was outside.

Betty went on her walk as planned, glad to be in the fresh air which was made extra pleasant as it was such a nice warm day. She bought a few purchases, including a small bottle of perfume as a present for her friend.

The warmth of the day made Betty feeling tired, which slowed her walk back to the Hall. If truth be known throughout most of the journey, Betty had been concerned about David and hoped he hadn't been working too hard which he often did especially of late. When she arrived back, she went straight back upstairs to David's study.

She found the door still shut. Betty still presumed David was working. She was just about to go back downstairs when she noticed a light flickering on and off from inside the room. Instinctively, Betty knew something was amiss and this was confirmed when she looked at the table outside the study door. The drink she had left there earlier remained untouched. By now, Betty felt rather agitated but thought the most likely explanation was that David was absorbed in his work. After knocking on the door several times she was disappointed there was still no reply.

'It's Betty, is everything alright, I've made you a drink?'

There was still no answer so she knocked again puzzled at the situation.

'It's Betty, open the door, it's nearly time for dinner. You've been working too hard.'

Still there was only silence. There was always the possibility that David had left his study and feeling tired had not seen the drink. Betty tried hard to open the door but found it was locked. David never locked his door when he was working but did so last thing at night. It was just something that he'd always done. He trusted his staff implicitly but at night he always said it was different and somebody could come into the house unawares. Luckily, there had never been any intruders and the Hall had always been safe but wisely David knew it was better to be cautious.

Betty stood unsure of what to do. She reasoned that the most likely explanation was that David had left the study and somehow the door was now jammed to. Minutes passed and Betty felt more in a quandary. She didn't want to worry anyone yet she knew to do nothing wasn't helping matters. Surely she thought to herself, David would have heard the knocking and unlock the door, unless he wasn't very well, in which case she knew she needed to get some help.

She quickly went down the stairs thinking herself foolish for her worries. It was as she walked down the main hall, that she noticed a car's headlights shining through the tall window at the end of the corridor. She peered through one of the long windows to get a better view and was surprised to see a car with its engine running. She instantly recognised the car from an article in The Times newspaper she'd read last month. It was a 20 HP Rolls Royce. David had the paper delivered every morning and Betty always made sure she found some time to have a quick read.

As she looked again the driver must have seen her and the car went off at speed down the main driveway, it's engine roaring. Betty knew that something wasn't quite right. Being Head of house, she was always informed of any visitors to the Hall and as far as she was concerned, nobody had visited the Hall that evening. She was puzzled just who the car belonged to and even more concerned by the driver's eagerness to leave the house so quickly.

Still deep in thought she almost bumped into George. He knew straight away she was upset.

'Whatever is the matter Betty?' he asked. 'What on earth has made you so upset?'

'It's David,' Betty said trying to catch her breath. 'Something is wrong, his study is locked and the drink I brought him earlier hasn't been touched,' she said her voice was now shaking as she spoke and she tried to take a deep breath to calm herself.

George listened carefully and was concerned himself by Betty's account.

'Don't worry Betty, I'll go and take a look, I'm sure it's nothing but it's better to be safe than sorry,' George said though he did not like the sound of the study door being locked but didn't want to unnecessarily worry Betty. She had been upset enough when he'd told her about Jimmy.

'I'm sorry to cause a fuss, but I'd be grateful if you could,' Betty said, sounding relieved. 'Since this wedding, all sorts of strange things have been happening. I don't like any of it, especially Albert. I've never told David my feelings as I felt it wasn't my place.'

'I'll handle this,' George said kindly aware that Betty was becoming more upset.

George was a considered man and he didn't want Betty to get carried away by emotion and say something against Bella that she might later regret. He'd had a worrying few weeks and was relieved that Jimmy was coming home and that he'd made a speedy recovery.

George quickly beckoned to one of the kitchen staff called Ted who was one of the younger members of the Hall who quickly got to his feet. Within a few minutes both men soon reached the study door and just as Betty had described, the door was locked.

'I must say, it's unusual for David to lock his study,' George said rather puzzled. 'Thankfully, I carry a spare key.'

He reached in his jacket pocket and produced a rather large looking set of keys. Rummaging through the keys, he eventually found the one he wanted and placed it in the lock to turn. Nothing happened. The lock was jammed and unable to rotate.

'Maybe it's a bit stiff,' he said more to himself than Ted. 'I suppose it's a long time since I've had to use this key. David only locks the study late at night and reopens it in the day.'

'Let's try again,' Ted said enthusiastically.

'Ok, you turn the key and I'll push the door as well,' George replied.

George put his body weight behind the door, pushing it with as much brute force as he had, whilst Ted attempted to turn the lock. It was useless, the lock was truly jammed.

Both men tried several more times but each time was in vain. George thought something on the inside of the door was blocking it or more importantly trying to stop anyone from the outside entering.

'Can we climb through a window?' Ted suggested aware that time was ticking on.

'No, I'm afraid we're too high up without a ladder and besides it's getting late, I'm afraid we've lost the light.' George pointed out looking at his watch. 'We need to get into that room quickly.'

'But how?' Ted asked in despair.

'I'm afraid it looks like we're going to have to break the door down,' George said. 'If David's in trouble we need to get in there as soon as possible.'

George looked around the corridor trying to find an object that could help push the door. He soon spotted an iron mantle left at the far side of the hall. Both men positioned themselves allowing their bodies to force the door open.

'Right, on my count of three,' George said hoping his plan would work.

'George before we begin, if the worst comes to the worst, how long would it take to get an ambulance here?'

'Too long, let's try and not think about that. Come on, let's try and be positive. We need to get in that room.'

Both men heaved with all their strength but the door wasn't budging.

'Keep trying,' George encouraged.

This time there was a little give which gave them some hope.

'I think if we push a few more times we might be lucky,' George said taking a deep breath.

It took however a further twenty attempts but eventually the door swung off its hinge. Cautiously, the two men peered in the room which was now in darkness. George remembered Betty had mentioned the study light being left on causing it to flash, yet somehow it mysteriously had been turned off. George felt the wall for a light switch, he pressed the switch but was surprised to find the bulb had been removed.

'Quick Ted, run to the store cupboard and grab a lantern,' said George who was becoming more suspicious.

Whilst Ted went downstairs, George cautiously entered the room, his eyes becoming more accustomed to the dark. Thankfully there was some light from the corridor which made it possible to just see the outline of shapes.

Firstly, George checked to see if David was at his desk, he couldn't see him so he moved further along the room still holding the fire mantle. He was more than aware somebody might still be in the room and at least he had some protection.

As George scanned the room, he noticed the window nearest the desk was open making the curtains swing from side to side. Otherwise there seemed to be nothing out of the ordinary but that didn't make him feel any better and George soon became aware of his own breathing which was becoming faster as his heart started to beat. Suddenly his foot hit something. The object felt hard and made him stop abruptly.

Having served in the trenches, George was not unfamiliar with dead bodies and knew exactly what his foot had touched. At that exact moment Ted rushed in the room bringing two other men.

'Quick over here,' George shouted. I've found a body, it's most likely to be David and it doesn't look good.'

Ted shone the gas lamp to the far side of the room. David lye motionless, his face staring up at the ceiling. His eyes cold and transfixed.

'Is he dead?' Ted asked nervously.

'I'm afraid so,' George whispered and went over to the body to check David's pulse. There was with no sign of life. 'It's useless, we can't help him.'

George closed David's eyes as a mark of respect but was careful not to disturb the body in any other way. A nasty feeling passed over him that almost seemed unthinkable. At this point, foul play could not be ruled out. A shiver went down George's spine. Betty was right the Hall had not been itself for a few months now and seemed full of secrets. None of which made any sense.

George broke the silence. 'Poor David, it's a very sad night for us all.'

'What do you think happened?' Ted asked who was showing signs of being in shock.

'It's difficult to say but I'm guessing he may have died some time ago. The body is fairly cold already.'

George had served in the war but no matter how many times he'd seen a dead body it still never came easy to him. Despite being upset, he surveyed the room, trying to piece together what may have happened. At first glance, nothing in the room looked as though it had been disturbed. George felt a loyalty to David and wanted to help but didn't know in the circumstances quite how to.

'I'll telephone the police, it's getting rather late so I doubt if they will come out this evening,' George said at last, trying to make sense of events.

'Do you think somebody did this to him?' Ted asked wanting to get out of the room quickly.

'I'm not sure yet,' George said truthfully.

'Or do you think he had a heart attack?'

'Maybe.' George stood up still never taking his eyes from the room. 'When the police arrive, they'll be able to tell us more.'

'Will you inform Mrs. Green?' Ted asked thoughtfully.

'Yes, though I think it might be wise to ask Betty to help me. I must confess, I'm not looking forward to this, Mr. and Mrs. Green have been married a long time. I don't quite know how she'll take such devastating news.'

By now, more lanterns were brought into the room which allowed George to have a good look at David. Making use of the light, he searched the room but there seemed no apparent sign of any disturbance. There was no evidence of any break in by somebody entering the room and on closer inspection of the body, there were no obvious signs of any wounds.

George couldn't help feel that something still didn't quite add up. Firstly, the study door being locked in the day was concerning. Looking up he noticed the light bulb had been removed from the room, probably deliberately by the looks of things. Betty had mentioned she had seen a flickering light in the room, maybe someone had removed the light as to not be seen.

Also suspiciously the study window had also been left wide open perhaps suggesting that someone had climbed in from the outside despite the room being quite high up. Sensibly George reasoned this could have been because David had opened it because of the warm weather they'd been having of late.

George closed the window with his handkerchief just in case the police wanted to examine the room and then shut the door. He walked towards the main parlour his mind confused with ideas. He felt something wasn't quite right about David's death and was determined for David's sake to find out exactly what had happened.

Betty Wilson had worked for the Green family for many years and could only cry when George sat her down to tell her the terrible news. To her it was unthinkable that Mr. Green was dead. She thought of him as fairly young for his age and knew that he kept himself fit playing tennis and golf in his spare time.

'I'm so sorry Betty, I know this is very difficult for you to take in.'

'He was as fit as a fiddle, I'm telling you, mind, he's not been himself recently and kept spending more time in his study,' sighed Betty in between crying and still trying to take in the dreadful news.

'I know it's a big shock for all of us to take in but I have to ask, will you come with me to break the news to Bella, Betty,' George asked. 'I'm sorry to ask you but I know she trusts you and I've got to be honest with you, I'm going to find this very difficult.'

Betty nodded her head. 'Of course, it needs to be done. We'll go now, it's best to get it over with, the poor woman will have to know sooner or later and it might as well be now.

'Thank you.'

'Just between you and me likes. What do you think happened to poor David?'

'I'm sorry but I'm not exactly sure,' George said honestly. 'But believe you me, we will find out.'

'You'll be needing to telephone Jimmy, thank goodness that son of yours is in the police.'

'He's coming to stay here but I'll ask him if he can come sooner.'

'It will be better when he's here with us,' Betty sighed.

'I'll telephone him later, but firstly let's find Bella, it's our duty to let her know.'

The pair found Bella sitting in the orangery at the back of the house. Betty couldn't help notice that she seemed already agitated and wondered if she knew of the news already. It was George who spoke first perhaps finding it easier from his time as a soldier.

'I'm very sorry Mrs. Green, I don't know how to say this, its bad news I'm afraid.'

Bella looked at George and there was a long silence.

'It's David, we couldn't get into his study this evening and when we did ... well I'm afraid we found that he was lying there on the floor, dead.'

Bella gasped and looked horrified.

'No,' she screamed. 'No, this can't be true. '

'Sadly, I'm afraid it is.'

George looked at Betty who so far looked too upset to speak.

George went on. 'We don't quite know the circumstances yet and naturally I took the liberty of phoning Whitby Police Station, in fact as we speak, they're sending some offices straight away.'

Bella looked devastated and George noticed a solitary tear roll down her face. It was as though she allowed herself that one tear but nothing else.

'Can I see him?'

Bella looked up and George took hold of her. She looked unsteady on her feet as though she might pass out through shock.

'I don't see why not but it's important that you don't disturb anything in the room until the police arrive,' George stressed.

'Of course,' Bella said at last. 'Thank you George.'

Bella looked at Betty who had now walked across the room to comfort her.

'It's truly dreadful,' Betty said to Bella. 'This is a terrible thing to happen.'

'I'm so sorry for what has happened to David. If you would like me to inform all the staff?' George asked politely.

'Please George, that would be very much appreciated,' Bella said, her voice faltering.

'When you're good and ready, we can make some plans for the necessary arrangements but clearly this is not the time,' Betty remarked thinking practically of all what was needed to be done.

'Yes, thank you Betty,' was all Bella managed to say sounding tired.

Bella was surprised by Betty's reaction thinking practically of the funeral arrangements but that was typical of Betty. It was obvious she was very upset yet here she was wanting to help with all the work that comes hand in hand with a death. Perhaps Bella already knew that David's death would inevitably make a huge ripple in terms of emotion and the amount of administration needed to be sorted.

'I feel as though I just need to see David,' Bella managed to say, her head already spinning with so many thoughts that it was impossible to think clearly. She wanted to go to her own room but knew the police would soon be arriving.

'By all means, take all the time you need, I don't think the police will get here within the hour, so if you go now, then…' his voice trailed off.

'Thank you both of you,' Bella said quietly and with that Bella went out of the room and headed for the stairs.

George's kind voice had a calming effect on Bella and she was grateful that she had been able to see David alone and spend a few precious moments with him. George had waited at the top of the corridor and could see that Bella looked physically and emotionally drained.

As they walked together down the stairs they could hear voices from the doorway. George had thought it necessary to contact the police immediately as soon as he had found David and from the voices, he assumed correctly that the police had just arrived and now more than anything he simply wanted to shield Bella from as many of the questions as possible. Death was never an easy subject.

# Chapter 14

Bella Green was a quiet woman by nature, so much so that her staff often complained that although they had worked for her for many years they still knew very little about her. George imagined right now she must want to be by herself in her own thoughts trying to make sense of what had happened. He regretted the fact that the police had arrived so soon but knew they needed to be contacted. At least David could now be taken to the chapel to be laid to rest.

'Thank you, Betty, that will be all.' Bella gestured as Betty left a large silver tray on the table with a pot of tea and four cups.

George sat with Bella at the far end of the room. The two officers introduced themselves as Inspector Jefferson and Hancock. Jefferson was the senior officer and immediately took charge. After nearly thirty years on the job, he had perfected a professional yet kind approach to interviews. His slightly bumbling attitude disguised a sharp alert mind. He seated himself on the large Chesterfield settee near the fireplace which had just been stoked.

'It's just a matter of a few questions Mrs. Green at this difficult time,' Jefferson said surveying the room and looking directly at Bella. 'Firstly, we're very sorry to hear about the sudden death of your husband Mr. Green. If it's alright with yourself, a few of my men are just in the study right now, we need to know exactly what happened this evening?'

'Yes, of course,' Bella said. 'Though I don't see how I can help.'

'Well that's our job and when we feel that we know exactly the cause of Mr. Green's death, we will of course inform you,' Jefferson said his manner blunt and then perhaps realising this, he softened his tone. 'I know all this must be terribly difficult for you but as you can see, we want to be able to give you some closure.'

'Yes, of course Inspector,' Bella sounded hoarse and she started to clear her throat.

'Nowadays, I'm afraid there's a lot of paperwork involved in the job you see,' Jefferson remarked.

He studied Bella as he talked and concluded that he didn't particularly like her, though he reasoned this didn't make her a cold blooded killer. At the moment the cause of death looked from natural causes. Still Jefferson remained suspicious after all that was his job. Bella fidgeted looking awkward but perhaps this was shock Jefferson thought.

'Yes, Inspector I quite understand, there's not such a lot I can tell you other than David had been working in his study while late in the afternoon. Betty went to take my husband a drink which he had asked for earlier. I believe she knocked on the door but David didn't answer so Betty simply left the drink on a nearby table.'

'At about what time was this?' Jefferson asked.

Bella thought carefully. 'I think it was about half past six but I can't be precise. Betty's such a dear, she makes it her duty to call on David if he's in his study but this evening she was a little late.'

'And why was that?' Jefferson questioned looking up from his note book.

'She was doing some errands for me,' Bella answered. 'She walked to the village. It's about an hour's walk away.'

'What sort of jobs?' the Inspector asked.

'Well, I had a few extra jobs for Betty, tidying up and that sort of thing, it's after the wedding, we've been so busy,' Bella said.

'Ah, yes that's the marriage of your daughter Mary Green and her new husband Albert Smithers?'

'Yes, as we speak, they're on their honeymoon in northern France, they're due to return the day after tomorrow,' Bella said sadly. 'I simply don't know how I will tell Mary, she will undoubtedly be devastated by such dreadful news.'

'All in good time,' the Inspector said writing quickly in his small note pad which he then placed on the table.

'As I was saying Inspector, I believe that Betty left David undisturbed as he doesn't like to be interrupted when he's working, so she knocked several times on the door and when he didn't answer, that's when she thought that something may be wrong,' Bella said trying to sound more confident than she felt.

'We will of course need to speak to Betty herself just to make sure we get all those minor details correct,' Jefferson said still quickly writing notes. 'By the way Mrs. Green, can I ask during all this time, where were you exactly in the house?'

Bella was surprised by such direct questioning. It was late and she felt in shock. 'Yes of course Inspector, I was sitting downstairs crocheting, currently I'm making a blanket for the church fete that's taking place in a few weeks.'

'So which room were you in at the time?'

'The sitting room which is at the back of the house, I keep a wooden cabinet that houses my sewing and haberdashery.'

'Right, I see, thank you, Mrs. Green. That will be all for now,' the Inspector said getting to his feet. 'I will really need to talk to Betty Wilson if that's alright with yourself?'

'Yes, of course.'

'Is there a room we can use to have a quick informal chat?'

'Yes, you can use the room just across the hall, we use it as a day room but there's a desk at the back, which might make things easier for you.'

'That would be fine. Can we speak with Mrs. Wilson right away, if that's convenient with yourself?'

'Yes, George will fetch her.'

As Betty Wilson waited for the Inspector, she couldn't help but fiddle with her thumbs rubbing them nervously together. She'd worked at the Hall for what seemed a good part of her life and was very close to David in fact she saw herself almost a mother figure to him. She tolerated Bella but thought her tone far too cold compared to her jovial husband who seemed to relish coming into the kitchens and on the odd occasion throughout the years had even made Sunday breakfast for some of the staff.

'There's nothing to be worried about Mrs. Wilson, we realise you're understandably in shock but we of course need to know exactly how Mr. Green died. Though it may be sad, it's part of our job and therefore we would like you to answer a few questions that we think are relevant to this case and it goes without saying that we really appreciate your time.'

'Well Inspector, I'm sorry but I really don't think I'm going to be much of a help.'

Betty's voice trembled and she would have liked George to be with her but knew that she had to be in the room alone and therefore felt quite intimidated by the officers.

'You just need to tell us what happened in the lead up to the events of Mr. Green's death?'

'Well now let me see...em... I had been talking to David, sorry that's Mr. Green and he'd asked for a cold drink to be taken upstairs to his study, it was a lemonade, there's nothing unusual about that. I then had a few hours to myself so I decided to go the local village, there's one or two nice little shops there, it's just outside the estate, only small mind but there's a lovely little shop that sells most things.'

'At about what time did you return?'

The Inspector was an impatient man and though he didn't want to rush Betty along he was quite abrupt in his manner and this understandably made Betty more nervous.

'I'd only been gone a couple of hours, it takes that time to walk there and back, you see I can't rush at my age, it's ever since I had problems with my knees and they've never been right since.'

'And then you came back to the Hall straight after that?'

'Yes, as I was about to say, I'd made sure before I left for the village that Mr. Green didn't need another drink. I knocked at the door but he didn't reply.'

The inspector pondered for a moment tapping his pen on the table. He knew it was common knowledge that David Green was a successful business man and at the moment, the most obvious cause of death was most likely that he'd suffered a major heart attack. Logically, he was after all middle aged and therefore it was notorious for men to suddenly to die from heart failure. Yet Jefferson hadn't been an Inspector for all these years to sense that something was amiss, as to what he hadn't worked that out yet, only time would tell.

'There's just one little thing I need to ask and then I think we're done here for the night?'

'What's that Inspector?' said Betty getting to her feet.

'I just need to clarify one small matter. Was the door to the study ever locked normally in the day?'

'That's the strangest thing, you see it never is in the day only in the evenings,' Betty said thoughtfully. 'It was so unlike Mr. Green, he didn't normally lock the door.'

'I see, could there be a reason?'

'Not that I can think of.' Betty shook her head. 'No, I can't think of any reason he would do that.'

'That's a very interesting point and may change things quite considerably,' the Inspector then paused. 'That will be all for now, I appreciate it's late so I wish you goodnight and thank you for your time Mrs. Wilson.'

'Yes and I'm sorry I can't be of more help,' Betty said feeling disappointed that she couldn't shed some light on the case.

'On the contrary, Mrs. Wilson, you have indeed been a useful help.'

Betty couldn't quite think how she might have been useful but smiled to the Inspector and bade him goodnight. Betty went downstairs and busied herself in the kitchens where she always felt safe. She had spent more time at the Hall since her husband had died several years earlier and David had been very kind to her at the time which had really helped her come to terms with her husband's death. She now wished she could do something for Bella and Mary that would help but she couldn't think of anything that would be appropriate. As she was deep in her thoughts, Bella came into the room looking worried and upset.

'Are you alright, my poor dear?' Betty said who was now also feeling quite tearful. 'This is a terrible time for Mary and yourself. But I can assure you that everyone at Herron Hall will be very saddened by Mr. Green's death, it is a ghastly thing to happen and a sad time for us all.'

'Oh, Betty thank you for your kind words,' Bella stopped talking and looked quite anxious.

'What is it?' Betty asked.

'It's the police... they have just informed me that they may have to do a post mortem.'

'Well, that's a thing.'

'Yes, quite,' Bella continued. 'Inspector Jefferson explained that it may after all be conceivable that David died not of heart failure but another cause of death.' Bella shifted uncomfortably before carrying on. 'They understand that the actual cause of death may be something else.'

'You mean someone murdered him?'

'I... I can't say. It's too much to think about,' Bella said putting her hands over her mouth.

'We must not think the worst yet,' Betty said trying to calm herself and Bella.

'Well, I don't understand, why would the police say such a thing?' Bella asked.

Betty turned to Bella trying to be as sympathetic as she could.

'Would you like me to do anything at all my dear, it's a truly terrible business that we find ourselves in. I just hope for all our sakes there's been no funny business,' Betty said. 'It makes me shiver to think if the Inspector is right in what he's saying then there's presence of evil all around us and God let it quickly be gone?' Betty said half whispering. 'I'm truly shaken by tonight's events.'

Betty looked at Bella, she knew this was going to be hard for her. She was trying to help and then she remembered that Jimmy would hopefully be arriving by the morning.

'Jimmy is coming to stay here tomorrow, I think he may be able to shed some light on the matter,' Betty said encouragingly.

'Oh, Jimmy I'd forgotten about him. Yes of course, George's son.'

Betty was surprised by Bella's tone. She sensed she didn't like Jimmy or was it because she thought he was beneath her. Betty knew she'd never liked Mary playing with him when they were younger. Bella was certainly a cold woman she thought.

Betty shuddered to think that perhaps there was something more sinister to David's death. It was a perishing thought to think that someone at the Hall could be involved. It was a thought that she quickly put aside. Yet she knew since the arrival of Albert, only trouble had followed. Betty felt she wouldn't sleep that night and reasoned that she might as well make a start to the following day's meals. If she started right away she could perhaps have a little nap later in the day.

Instinctively she started to pour the ingredients of a cake mixture she wanted to make into the baking bowl for tomorrow's lunch. As the ingredients began to gather in the bowl, Betty thought the mixture of so many foods seemed a good analogy for the turmoil of tonight's events. She was so deep in thought that she was startled by a loud noise coming from behind her and turned quickly. She felt a little foolish when she realised it was only Bella who had now come back in the room.

'Eh, I'm sorry to be so jumpy,' Betty said at last.

'Of course it's only natural to feel like that. For what it's worth, I feel exactly the same.'

Betty continued stirring the cake mixture. 'When will you be letting dear Mary know?' Betty asked aware of the quietness of the room.

Betty didn't really want to pry but it was important to think practically and Mary had a right to know as soon as possible about her father's death.

'I thought it best to wait until the morning,' Bella said. 'I very much doubt I would even get through on the phone line this time of night but I would like her to know fairly soon. In fairness she will be home tomorrow but I need to tell her before.'

'Yes. It will be hard for you. '

'Yes.' Bella said quietly.

'I think perhaps you should be turning in. You've had a nasty shock,' Betty said. 'Would you like me to pour you a night cap to help you through the night?'

'No, but that's very kind. I don't quite know how I'm going to tell Mary.'

'Well she's very close to David, it's not going to be easy for her.' Betty said. 'Mind your Mary's always been a strong girl, she'll figure something out and besides now she's got Albert to take care of her. At least she's married and it won't be as hard as being on her own.'

Betty looked at Bella trying to reassure her but Bella only looked coldly back.

# Chapter 15

Edward had been thinking about Jimmy all week. By all accounts from speaking to George over the phone, Jimmy by some miracle looked remarkably well for a man that had been shot twice in the chest. Despite having sustained such serious injuries, thankfully he'd made a good recovery. Edward felt relieved and even more so knowing that he was back at Herron Hall. It had been a close call for Jimmy but he was young and fit, which had helped him pull through.

Edward had just arrived home and stood on his drive reaching for his briefcase. For once the train from London had made good time and Edward was looking forward to spending the evening with his family. The following week, he'd arranged to travel up to Herron Hall to spend some time with Mary and David so for now he wanted to make the most of his time at home.

As he opened the porch door, the first thing Edward noticed was how upset Verity looked as though she'd been crying and immediately Edward thought it was because of one of the children.

'What is it Verity, tell me?' Edward asked wondering what could have happened.

'It's David, I don't know how to say this but... he's dead,' Verity said quietly, her voice was hoarse as though she was struggling to say the words out loud.

'What...that can't be, for heavens sake, I talked to him ... well just a few weeks ago. When did this happen?' Edward couldn't quite believe the news.

'Bella phoned me a couple of hours ago, they think it was a heart attack of some kind but the police are carrying out a post mortem anyway to find out the exact cause of death.'

'I can't believe this, it's a complete shock and so sudden. How's Bella taken the news?' was all Edward managed to say, his head whirling from the sequel of events which had occurred recently.

'She sounded terribly upset but more importantly, she's dreading telling Mary. She and Albert are back from their honeymoon later tonight. You know she's very close to David and she won't take the news well and Bella knows that.'

Verity slid her arm into Edward's and led him to the house while the taxi went slowly down the drive. Edward suddenly stopped in his tracks.

'Verity.'

'What is it Edward?'

'I think something terrible is going on, remember I mentioned a while ago that David was having doubts about the Smithers' family and in the end as the weeks went by, he was absolutely against the marriage fearing that Albert had only chosen Mary for her money.'

'Yes, but they're married now and I hate to point out, but it's David that's dead not Mary, what possible gain would that be for Albert?' Verity said carefully choosing her words, aware that Edward looked tired and she wanted him to sit down with a drink. 'Think about it Edward, if there was any funny business, it would be Mary not David they would kill.'

'But that's just it, Verity. First the attempt on Jimmy's life. For heaven's sakes he was shot only a few weeks ago. At the time as far as I know he was acting on some information about Albert Smithers.'

'I know it doesn't sound good but you've got to keep a clear head and think rationally,' Verity said aware of how Edward must be feeling.

'It's a miracle that Jimmy is alive. He's so brave, thank goodness he managed to shoot the man in self defence,' Edward said allowing himself time to think. 'Let's face it, if he'd not been found more or less straight away, he'd have bled to death. Now David is dead, surely it's not just a coincidence.'

By now Verity and Edward had walked into the drawing room and Edward poured himself a whisky his hands shaking as he did so.

'I'm so sorry to hear this dreadful news,' Verity said sadly.'I know how close you were to David, it's a real blow to us all.'

'Yes, but don't you see, Jimmy was shot for acting on information from me about Albert and now what with David found dead in his study, Verity none of this makes sense and I know for certain I'm overlooking something,' Edward said staring into his drink to try to make some sense of what seemed a catalogue of events that didn't quite fit together.

'But do you really think Albert would kill David and besides you're missing the fact that Bella said it's likely he suffered a heart attack and at this stage nobody thinks he's been murdered.'

'I know but is that for certain?' Edward asked his hands still slightly shaking.

'Well, now you come to mention it, perhaps Bella did say the Police wanted to carry out a post mortem,' Verity said still horrified by the sad news. 'But I think it's just routine.'

'Not necessarily,' Edward said. 'Verity, it's sounds to me as though the police are not exactly sure as to just what happened to David, there's a degree of uncertainty and that's not good.'

'I still think it's probably procedure. Your brother after all is a very wealthy successful man.'

'Yes.'

'Look Edward, I agree with you. Poor David's death looks slightly suspicious to say the least but it could just be coincidental,' Verity said slowly then smiled to herself.

'Maybe.'

'Oh, for goodness sake Edward, you're the solicitor and you're always telling me to only deal in facts. Let's face it, Jimmy's life is half in the east side of London, most days mixing with the very scum of society. I bet over the years he must have made plenty of enemies, just think how many people he's arrested. I'd say it's understandable, I'm sorry but it's just the way it is.'

'You could be right.'

'Yes, everybody knows that police work, well it's a precarious profession and unfortunately David is at an age where heart attacks are common ...why you only mentioned a few weeks ago that a colleague died at work. I'm afraid it's not that uncommon.'

'Yes, but David dead, it doesn't seem right.'

'I'm sorry but David, didn't look the fittest of men despite the fact he enjoyed playing tennis,' suggested Verity trying to think practically without being hurtful.

'I just don't like it Verity and it's not like Bella and Mary are here safe and sound where it's easier to keep an eye on them. They live the other side of the country, in some bleak remote place, that half the time is that damned foggy you can't see anything.'

Verity laughed. Edward thought anywhere outside of London was farmland. If truth be known, he'd have much preferred to live in London itself rather than where they currently lived on the outskirts but when the twins had been born, he'd softened somewhat to country life.

'Look, this is what we'll do,' Verity said taking charge. 'Firstly, you must telephone Bella and convey our sympathies. She has a very difficult time ahead of her and she will want all the help she can get.'

'I will,' Edward said slowly getting to his feet. He felt in deep shock. 'In fact, that's exactly what I'll do.'

# Chapter 16

Edward slowly put the receiver down. It had been the fifth time he'd tried to telephone the Hall that evening but on each occasion there had been no answer. Naturally, Edward was feeling extremely upset and all sorts of thoughts started to go through his mind. He imagined Bella isolated in the Hall. He consoled himself that both George and now Jimmy were there and hopefully would keep her safe. Mary would also now be back at home having travelled from France and he wondered just how she'd taken the terrible news.

He tried one last time and was rewarded. At last the receiver was picked up and Bella came onto the line. He was relieved to hear her voice though the crackly line made her sound terribly faint.

'It's me Bella, how are you holding up?'

'I'm as good as to be expected Edward, it's devastating news, I simply can't believe David is dead, it came right out of the blue I'm afraid. I've told Mary and Albert, poor girl she was always a bit of a daddy's girl and she'll so miss him.'

'How are you?' Edward asked feeling hopeless on the other end of the line. He wanted to ask Bella if he thought there was something more sinister to David's death. This however didn't seem appropriate on the telephone, it was too soon. Bella understandably had hundreds of things on her mind and during the somewhat brief conversation Edward couldn't find the right words to tell her his thoughts.

'Bella I've decided to come up for a few days to help out,' Edward blurted out. He planned to do this anyway and he knew David would have wanted him to take care of his family.

'Edward that's awfully kind of you to offer but it's not necessary at all and besides I've got Albert and Mary and there's nothing you can do here, sit tight and I'll let you know when I have any news. I have to go now my dear as Betty wants me. I'll speak soon, good bye.'

The receiver went abruptly down before Edward had even chance to say good bye. Edward couldn't help but feel that things must be worse than Bella was letting on. Edward remembered Detective Howarth's contact details which he still had in his jacket pocket. He looked at the clock at the far side of the room, it was gone nine so he doubted there would be any answer on the other end of the line but he wanted some reassurance. Howarth had been very persistent when he told Edward to contact him with any news.

As the evening passed the lights of the train had dimmed and the carriages were rattling past villages and a few small towns that could be seen on the skyline, their street lights shining.

'So, what did Edward do, did he go back to Herron Hall?' asked Sophie who'd so far been mesmerised by the story.

'Well, let me think. Oh, my legs are beginning to stiffen, it's old age setting in,' Emily laughed. 'From what I can remember the train waits at the next station for a while. I reckon after that we've only got about an hour left to Hull,' Emily pointed out.

'So, did Edward go back to Herron Hall in the end? ' Sophie asked again.

'Well, let me see...' Emily said thoughtfully whilst twisting the end of her spectacles in her mouth.

Soon the train had reached the end of the next tunnel and Emily continued to recount the story. So, it was that as tunnels passed and railway sidings, the story itself unravelled with its many twists and turns.

'You see, Edward had been somewhat perturbed by his conversation with Bella. He still was reeling over what had happened to Jimmy and then the death of David. It had been a horrendous day and he felt in shock.

There was also something bothering him and that was Bella, she was obviously grieving far more than he had initially thought. He impulsively knew he must go to Herron

124

Hall and that time was of an essence. Firstly, though he decided to telephone Howarth but before he could do so, Verity stepped into the room.

'It's Detective Howarth on the line for you, shall I tell him to call you back?'

Edward took a deep breath. 'I think I should speak to Howarth now, it's better to get it over and done with.'

'Superintendent Inspector Howarth, is that you, the telephone line isn't too clear but I hear you have some news?'

'Is this a good time to talk?'

'Yes, but it just so happens that you've caught me at a very bad time,' Edward said truthfully wondering what the Detective was going to say. At the same time he was also relieved he'd contacted him. He wondered if he knew about David.

'Mr. Green, firstly I'm very sorry to hear about your brother and offer my sincere condolences to both yourself and your family.'

'Thank you. I'm just devastated,' Edward managed to say quietly. 'Bella believes David died of a heart attack.'

'And what do you think?'

'I'm not so sure,' Edward said honestly. 'Do you think there's more to the story and it could be foul play?'

'I see, I think it's too early to make any judgements at this stage,' Howarth said and then changed the subject. 'Herron Hall is near Whitby and therefore as I understand it, the case will be in the hands of our friends in the North Yorkshire Constabulary under the watchful eye of an Inspector Dudley,' Howarth said thinking how the story was fitting together. 'Though now Jimmy has nearly recovered I believe he's up there too. He's not fit for duty yet but still he's a valuable help.'

'Yes, in some ways I'm glad he's there to keep an eye on Mary,' Edward remarked. 'By the way, have you had Albert in for questioning yet only I have to say that Jimmy mentioned to me that he believed James and Albert could be involved in smuggling goods in and out of the country?'

Edward asked impatiently, he was keen now to get some answers.

'Well... that's interesting. I can't discuss the particulars of the case of course but what I can tell you that we've had his father in for lengthy questioning.'

'James?'

'Yes.'

'What did he say?'

'Not a great deal. Because of your profession, I'm sure you're more than aware it's not easy to go pointing the finger of blame. We've got to tread carefully and that will be difficult.'

'There must be something you can do, surely...?'

'Going back to the evening you met Jimmy, what exactly did he tell you?' Howarth asked.

'Only that he thought James and Albert were involved in unscrupulous dealings of sorts,' Edward said wishing now he had kept this information to himself and not let his thoughts run away with him.

'I can assure you that both Albert and his father have of course denied any such wrong doings. At this present time, I'm afraid there's not a scratch of evidence to link them to any smuggling or racketeering of any kind.'

'That's a real shame.'

'I can tell you this however,' Howarth continued. 'Both men cover their tracks well.' Howarth paused as if trying to think what he was going to say next. 'I'm afraid it's a matter of catching them red handed so to speak.'

'Of course, I understand.'

'It's important that you leave all police business to us. I realise you're only trying to help but sometimes things get out of hand and people can get hurt.'

Edward didn't like the sound of this and it made him think immediately of his friend.

'What about the attack on Jimmy?' asked Edward, again he was feeling frustrated by how slowly the law worked.

'At the moment, there's no circumstantial evidence to link father and son to anything underhand, they are still acting within the law,' Howarth sighed. 'I'm sorry Mr. Green but at this stage of the enquiry unfortunately we have our hands tied. You of course have my absolute reassurance that we're doing everything we possibly can and you have my word that I personally have taken a very keen interest in this case.'

'Yes, that reassures me, it's all very difficult, I do understand,' Edward said considerately.

Edward privately thought this flimsy explanation for not arresting James or Albert and bore no reflection to the severity of the case. The truth of the matter was that Jimmy had been shot and had just arrived home from a few weeks spent recovering in hospital.

Howarth went on. 'It's all hearsay of Jimmy who having been shot was found next to the body of some unknown petty criminal, who I might add, the man's record with the police can only reveal acts of theft in and around Petticoat Lane Market. There is absolutely no connection to Albert or James. This conclusion, I'm afraid is simply not enough to bring a case against them so unless I have something concrete.' Howarth paused sensing Edward's disappointment. 'I understand your frustration and I'll get straight on to the Whitby constabulary.'

'Of course.'

'Let's see what the post mortem brings. You've got to be patient Mr. Green. The law works slowly, you of all people should know that.'

'That's what bothers me, we may not have time on our side, all of this doesn't add up, I know there's something else.'

'Leave it to us now, thank you your help with the information regarding your brother, although obviously I can assure you I'll be very much up to date on aspects of this case from now on. We have at this stage got to let our friends in Whitby do their job.'

'Yes, I understand.'

'Good, then I'll make some enquiries with their Inspector and tell him about both James and Albert and what happened to Jimmy but at this stage we can't treat anything that has happened to your brother with any suspicion, I'm afraid it all rests on the autopsy. I'll tell you what, as a favour I'll phone some friends and see if we can rush things through.'

Howarth was trying to sound fair but Edward felt disappointed how matters had been handled so far, it all sounded good but nothing had reassured him that a full investigation was happening.

'Let's see what happens, I just think it's very suspicious, that's all,' Edward repeated.

'I agree but suspicion is not enough to go on.'

# Chapter 17

Kings Cross Station on a Friday morning was always busy and Edward had been lucky to get a ticket let alone first class which he regarded as essential for the length of journey up to Hull. He'd packed a small suitcase enough for a few days with a formal jacket and tie if needed. The funeral arrangements were for a few weeks when he would return with his family.

Usually Edward enjoyed taking the train up the country but this time he felt tense. He didn't know what to expect and there was a strong possibility he could be walking into something that he didn't want to.

On the other hand, Bella and Mary would be alone suffering and would need even practical help with all the finances regarding David's estate. The other pressing reason for this sudden visit was Edward thought there could be a real danger that Mary his niece was in trouble and for that very reason, Edward had made the decision to travel to Whitby.

Mary had only a few relations that she could turn to. Edward suspected Mary didn't really know her mother's side of the family that well and on David's side of the family apart from himself, all of her relations lived in America which right now seemed very far away.

When the train pulled into one of the stations further north, luckily a lot of passengers got off the train which immediately altered the mood of the journey making it far more relaxing and more importantly giving Edward a chance to think. He felt exhausted but tried to clear his mind and think logically about everything that had happened.

When he arrived at Whitby, Bella was now expecting him having telephoned her but he'd not specified a time just in case of a late arrival. He'd told her that he would call from the station in Whitby and then from there he'd catch a taxi to Herron Hall.

Eventually the small commuter train pulled into the small station of Whitby. It had up till now been a warm day and the cold breeze that blew in from the North Sea brought with it a heavy sea mist. It had become so dense, Edward couldn't even see the shape of the iconic Abbey. The mist seemed like a blanket disguising the landscape.

After a few minutes, Edward managed to get himself a taxi to take him to the Hall. This had proved to be more difficult than he had anticipated as the station seemed eerily quiet. Edward was starting to get cold when at last a taxi pulled up. Despite having to pay double the going rate for the taxi fare, he was relieved at last to be seated in relative warmth heading down country narrow roads.

Judging from his past visits he calculated that it usually took about twenty minute to drive from Whitby itself to the Hall. Probably due to the sea fret or the driver's lack of local knowledge of the area, it took the greater part of an hour before he finally arrived.

The Hall looked very different from his last visit for Mary's wedding when he had stayed with Verity and their children. It confirmed Edward's beliefs that the coast could be very deceptive, looking its best on a nice summer's day but if the weather changed, then the entire mood of the place did as well but never so much he thought to himself as it did tonight.

As the car pulled up the long drive, the Hall was entirely shrouded in mist and the effect was to send a shiver down Edward's spine. George thankfully greeted him standing at the main entrance to the house and came to take his suitcase and just as he stepped inside he saw Jimmy. He looked far slimmer than the last time he saw him and had a sling across his arm but all things considered, he looked remarkably well and more importantly had survived by some miracle of fate.

'Jimmy, I'm so pleased to see you,' Edward said greeting his friend with a firm shake of the hand.

'I'm so sorry about David, father told me all about it. It's a great blow to all of us. My father is quite shocked by the events that have happened. It's simply awful,' Jimmy responded shaking his head in disbelief.

'Absolutely. We've got things to discuss.'

'It's truly been a terrible time,' said Jimmy addressing Edward again.

'How are Bella and Mary holding up, I would very much like to see Bella to offer my condolences?'

'They're as good as to be expected in the circumstances, very up and down I would say but as I've said, it's to be expected,' Jimmy said. 'You know how good David has been to my family and he has always really helped me from being a young boy.'

'My brother always thought of all his staff as family and so do I,' Edward said truthfully.

'It's a great loss. Bella is waiting in the front parlour. Mary is there too,' Jimmy explained. 'But first.' Jimmy looked around to see if anybody was around. 'I don't believe for one second David suffered a heart attack. I've racked my brains to think what actually happened. My father assures me that the door of the study was locked yet we know David never locked the door until late evening.'

'Are you sure about that?'

'Yes, call it gut instincts but I think somebody wanted David out of the way.'

Edward looked at Jimmy. He trusted his sharp mind. He'd not got to be an Inspector in such a short space of time for no reason.'

'What are you saying?' Edward asked his mind quickly thinking ahead.

'I'm thinking foul play is at stake.' Jimmy lowered his voice.

'I think you're right. But what's to be done? Poor Mary. Albert surely has something to do with this.'

'We can't accuse him and besides you're not officially on the case,' Edward pointed out.

'That's perhaps to our advantage, as I can observe from afar.'

Suddenly they were aware of footsteps behind them, it was Betty.

'Edward how lovely to see you,' she said. 'Thank goodness you're here.'

'Likewise, though I wish my visit could be in happier circumstances.'

'There's a late dinner for you. You'll naturally be tired after such a journey. It is after all a particularly foul evening.'

'Yes.'

'Well do go on through to the front drawing room where there is a small table ready for you with some good hearty food.'

'Thank you, Betty, that's very kind.'

'How is Mary?' Edward quizzed.

'She's sleeping now but she'll be really pleased to see you in the morning.'

Edward followed Betty down the corridor which led into the front parlour. He was surprised to find Bella sitting by the window. The room was dark and cold a lot like Bella Edward thought.

'I'm so glad you've managed to come Edward,' Bella said and squeezed Edward's hand which seemed oddly out of character. 'Firstly though after your long train journey you must eat.'

Edward was pleased to see a tray full of delicious looking food. A meat pie with potatoes and vegetables sat neatly served on a rather large plate. He remembered just what a good cook Betty was and now ravenously hungry, he quickly sat to eat.

As Edward ate he couldn't help thinking how tired and worried Bella looked. Her eyes were sore and swollen as though she had been crying a great deal. Yet the Bella he had spoken to on the phone had seemed unemotional and cold. Perhaps Bella was more upset than he initially thought and maybe she was suffering from shock Edward thought to himself.

Edward made some small talk with Bella but otherwise there was an awkward silence between them. Thankfully there was a knock on the door and Betty came to take the tray.

'Thank you, Betty that will be all,' said Bella addressing her with a smile, Betty quickly left closing the door behind her leaving Bella and Edward once more alone. Edward sat for a while wanting to ask questions but at the same time, he hated having to push Bella for answers but he needed to get some clarity.

'Bella forgive me for being so forward but has it crossed your mind that perhaps David's death was suspicious?'

'Is that what you think?'

'I'm not sure.' Edward paused then went on. 'Do you think Albert and James are somehow behind this?'

Bella looked shocked and was obviously surprised by Edward's suggestion. Instantly Edward wished he hadn't been quite so bold with his questioning, but after all it was a difficult subject to broach. He also knew the police would only be asking the same. He reasoned it was far better the questions coming from him than being interrogated by the local constabulary.

'Bella I know it's a difficult time for you,' Edward said sympathetically. 'But right now we have to think of what could and may have happened?'

Bella sat still not answering. She looked deathly pale and Edward wondered if she had taken tablets to calm herself.

'No,' came the answer. 'I don't think so Edward but ... the police aren't so sure, tomorrow they've informed me they will be carrying out the post mortem. I suppose then we will get to know exactly what did happen.' Bella explained, her cheeks gaining some colour. Edward noticed she instinctively tightened the scarf she was wearing.

'Bella the police will ask you if you saw anything suspicious or you thought odd on the night of David's death?' Edward paused. 'Try and think carefully as the police will want to know, even a little detail may prove to be important.'

'No, that night there was nothing out of the ordinary,' Bella said looking at Edward as though studying him. 'I've given the matter a great deal of thought, in fact Edward to tell you the truth I can't stop thinking about it, I just keep going through it over and over again in my mind. I can assure you though nothing out of the ordinary happened that evening.'

'I'm sorry to ask.'

'Between you and me I think David had been working too hard. He always has, it was just one of those things that made David who he was,' Bella said.

'Yes, his work meant a lot to him,' Edward agreed.

'You know David probably better than anyone and you know how he was, he always lived life to the full, that was just his nature.'

'And Mary, how is she?' Edward asked wondering how she had taken the news.

'Obviously she's not at her greatest but Albert has been very good to her and she seems up until now to be coping but it's early days. I know David had doubts about Albert but I think David may have misjudged Albert.'

Edward raised his eyes.

'Edward, he's actually been very kind and sweet to my dear Mary.'

Edward was rather taken aback by this change of heart but perhaps this was still the shock of David's death making Bella too confused to think carefully. Bella's sentiments didn't sway Edwards thoughts. He wanted explanations, there was something suspicious going on and he was intent on finding out what.

'Look Bella,' Edward said putting his hand over hers. 'I have it on very good authority that both Albert and James have been...'.

'Yes.'

'Well, it's a delicate matter and I haven't wanted to tell you but this is as good a time as any.'

It was difficult to judge Bella's mood and Edward didn't want to upset her any more than he had to but this situation was getting out of hand and quite frankly he thought Bella had subsequently gone into some sort of self denial about Albert. She now needed to be told just what he was capable of.

Edward went on. 'Bella, I feel I have a right to tell you that there is a possibility that both James and Albert are somehow involved in unscrupulous dealings that may bring terrible repercussions for yourself and Mary.'

'You're surely mistaken.'

'I'm afraid not.'

'Will they be arrested?'

'At the moment, it seems unlikely, you see there is no concrete evidence to be able to arrest them. For now it's only speculation and as it is, these insinuations would be thrown straight out of court. James and Albert cover their tracks well. It would seem they still have friends in high places, enough at least to get them out of trouble.'

Bella looked shocked. Edward knew however, he had done the right thing. It was necessary to put her in the picture, it was about time.

'No Edward, you're mistaken, it can't be true as we'd have heard something on the grapevine, no one gets away with anything in our circles without somebody hearing something about it, you're mistaken Edward,' Bella exclaimed looking confused and upset at Edward's accusations.

'A friend of mine was nearly killed finding this out,' Edward said realising that Bella didn't want to hear the truth, he decided not to tell her about Jimmy. He'd been careful not to mention why he'd been shot. Edward knew better than to say anything that could implement Jimmy.

'What do you mean, when was this, why didn't you tell me?'

Edward could see that Bella was clearly upset and this was the last thing she wanted to hear right now.

'Thankfully it appears that he was spared and it seems that he's now luckily out of danger.'

Bella took out a cigarette which shocked Edward, in all the years he'd known her, he'd never seen her smoking and wondered if she always had.

'Is the chap in question young Jimmy?' Bella enquired inhaling on the cigarette.

'That's right,' Edward said surprised by Bella's knowledge. How would she know this he thought to himself. 'He's damned lucky to be alive I say.'

'So it was Jimmy,' Bella said smiling to herself. I'm sorry Edward but I still think this is all very fanciful, whatever next. No Edward you cannot expect me to believe such cobblers.'

'Bella, there's a very good chance what I'm telling you is true.' Edward drew a breath. 'If it is, then that could explain David's death and it also alerts me to another problem in fact two and that's why I'm here,' Edward explained.

'What's that?' asked Bella a little frustrated by Edward's reluctance to listen to her point of view.

'It's you and Mary, you both could be in terrible danger. '

Bella laughed out loud. 'What a load of tommy rot, this is getting to be absurd Edward. David told me that you've always had a vivid imagination at the best of times but this is just verging on being ridiculous,' Bella laughed stubbing out her cigarette in an ashtray on a nearby table.

Edward had finished his dinner by now and was grateful for such lovely food but he feared he'd over stepped the mark and wanted to excuse himself to go in his room.

'It's late Bella, I'm sorry if I've upset you but if you don't mind I'm pretty tired and if I could go to my room which I presume is upstairs.'

'Of course,' Bella said getting up almost forgetting her manners. 'It's the room that you always stay in. Look, I'm afraid we're all on tender hooks here and we'll talk more about this in the morning.'

'Thank you, Bella and good night.'

Edward kissed Bella on the cheek and went upstairs to his room. Eventually exhaustion gave way to Edward's troubled mind and he was soon fast asleep. He surprised himself by not waking until mid morning. After eating breakfast, he read the morning papers which seemed to be full of doom with respect to share prices around the major markets of the world but he observed none too much to cause any real trouble to any one single economy. Suddenly the door opened and Bella came into the room looking anxious.

'Last night after you went to bed I couldn't sleep and lay awake worrying about what you had told me about David. I thought I'd go upstairs to his study, you see I knew he kept a secret safe in the wall by the window.'

Edward was surprised by this and wondered what Bella had found that had made her look so worried.

'Do the police know about this?' Edward asked keen for Bella to tell him more.

'No, I think it's best that …' Bella paused and looked at Edward as though she was finding the right words. 'I think it's best if we keep the safe a secret,' Bella said thoughtfully.

'Listen Bella you need to tell me exactly what you've found, withholding evidence could incriminate yourself, the police won't look favourably to that if it ever came out at a later stage.'

'I can do better than that, I'll show you but I don't think you'll like what I've found,' Bella hesitated. 'I think you'd better have a look all the same,' said Bella reluctantly handing Edward the envelope which was quite heavy and looked to contain several sheets of letters inside. Edward emptied the contents and a single sheet of paper landed on the table next to where Edward was seated. Edward saw at once that it was his brother's handwriting.

'Can I read it?' he asked.

'Yes, I think you need to take a look.'

Edward looked at the sheet that was slightly crumpled and started to read the letter. The handwriting was small and slightly smudged in places but Edward managed to read most of it, at least enough to get the general gist.

'Gracious Bella, it's David's suicide note and by the looks of it…' he said and paused. 'This has been written a while ago, I suppose at least this tells us what may have happened.'

Edward held the paper for a moment trying to understand what David had been going through, to take his own life was such a serious act and suddenly Edward felt guilty that he'd not been there for his brother. He'd been so busy with his own life and building up his career. Bella stood there quietly and let Edward get his breath back.

'Bella, we need to tell the police about this, I've been liaising with Superintendent Howarth, he needs to read this, you understand, don't you?'

Edward knew he had to convince Bella to do the right thing. Bella looked at Edward and at last nodded.

'Alright but this needs to be handled delicately, we also have to think of the family name, suicide doesn't look good but I suppose we all belong to the Smithers' family don't we,' she said with a degree of sarcasm in her voice which took Edward by surprise.

'I'll get right onto it.'

Edward smiled sympathetically. Things were moving quickly and he hoped for both Bella and Mary's sake that he could somehow halt the tide of pain for both of them. Bella walked out of the room but as soon as she went, Edward thought about the handwriting he'd just seen and that's when he knew that it wasn't David's. The handwriting that Bella had just shown him sloped to the right and as David was left handed, David's writing sloped to the left. It was just something he'd always been aware of as he remembered back to his school days. Edward had been praised for his handwriting and told that it didn't slope unlike his older brother. At the time, it had pleased Edward as he had always been in awe of David and it was nice to know that his handwriting was far the better of the two.

The handwriting was a minor detail but as far as Edward was concerned it was a major one. One thing he'd learnt studying the law was that the devil is in the detail. It's never the big ideas, on the contrary it's always the small ones that say so much. He also must tell Jimmy. They'd so far not had time to discuss matters. Minutes later Edward headed down the corridor which led to Jimmy's room. Thankfully the door was open and Jimmy looked relieved to see him as he beckoned him inside.

'Shut the door.'

'Jimmy, I'm afraid I have bad news, Bella has just confronted me with a letter from David.'

'What did it say?' Jimmy asked who was thankfully looking more like his old self.

'It was David's suicide note.'

'David...you've got to be joking?'

'Well I confess initially to believing this to be true but the more I think about this absurd idea the more I don't believe David did this. You see the handwriting that Bella shown me, it wasn't David's.'

'Are you sure about that?'

'Yes. I'm totally sure.'

'This doesn't make sense. Why would Bella not know, do you think she is lying?'

'That's the thing. I honestly don't know. Jimmy what do you think is going on here?'

'My father tells me that there's been a few shenanigans happening of late, for example the night of David's death, Betty told him about a car she'd seen coming from the drive. I'm inclined to believe that David was murdered. As for who did it, I've yet to figure that out. Officially I'm not here on police duty and I have to tread carefully. I think you'd better let Howarth know about the suicide letter. He'll be surprised to find out that David didn't write it. This certainly sheds some light on the case. We need to keep him in the loop.'

'Yes of course,' Edward said still concerned about the handwriting. 'I want you to keep an eye on Mary.'

'Believe me I am,' Jimmy sighed. 'Though it's been difficult. Albert seems to keep her on a tight reign. I really do not like him.'

'Join the long line,' Edward smiled, he appreciated Jimmy's honesty.

'Keep in touch, if I hear any news I'll keep you posted.'

'Likewise.'

The fog was playing havoc with the phone lines that evening and Edward had to wait a good hour before being put through. The line was still crackly and Edward was surprised when Howarth answered straight away.

'Good Evening. It seems there's been developments. I have some news for you,' Howarth said down the line. 'I'm afraid the situation is more serious than we first thought. In fact I've deemed it necessary to travel up to Whitby. I shall be arriving at Herron Hall early tomorrow.'

'I'd no idea you'd be coming to Whitby,' Edward said wondering exactly what was going on.

'Yes, as you're aware, I'm solely responsible for this case and I've taken it upon myself to make sure Bella and Mary are safe. I therefore will travel from London, a very long journey I might add. As I've said, there's been important developments and I think I may have stumbled on to something.'

'Right. What exactly?'

'I'm afraid we're now talking first degree murder. We have evidence that David didn't die of a heart attack as we first suspected, he was poisoned, it looks like it went straight to the heart. I guess it would have killed him within minutes which is some consolation but nevertheless, I have to say, a nasty death at the best of times and from what we can see from the investigation so far, someone gave him double the dosage. Put it this way whoever wanted him dead wasn't taking any chances.'

Although Edward had suspected foul play it was still a shock to him, the poisoning of David and secondly the incident with Jimmy in London. If this was Smithers' work then he was a far bigger player than he'd first suspected.

'I can't say I'm altogether surprised as I already had my suspicions. There's something else you need to know,' Edward said keen to share the business of the suicide note

140

with Howarth. 'David kept a secret safe in the wall of his study, I don't quite know how but Bella managed to have the code but nevertheless she opened it and has taken some of the papers. It would seem within some of the papers was a suicide note, which I know for certain was not genuine but a fake. Surely after what you've just told, it proves that it definitely is …' Edward paused waiting for Howarth to respond. 'Murder, it's got to be murder?'

'Sadly yes and from what you've just told me it now seems Bella is not telling us the whole truth, I wonder what she is hiding?'

'I'm not sure,' Edward replied.

'Yes, this is very interesting news, is there anything in the note that leads us to Albert?' Howarth asked.

'I've read the note and it wasn't my brother's handwriting, I know that because he was left handed and his writing from being a young boy always sloped to the left not the right.'

'That's interesting.'

Edward hated to say it but he wasn't a man to mince his words. 'Do you think that Bella is somehow involved? ' Edward asked not sure of what response he would receive.

'Well I think not but this puts a whole new slant on the case and I certainly will be having words when I see that sister in law of yours as withholding information is something the police don't look too kindly on. I will be asking some serious questions,' Howarth paused. 'As I've previously told you, I have a very keen interest in this case you have my word for that.'

'Yes and I'm grateful for that. I guess it's also necessary to take into consideration that Bella is scared and doesn't know what to do for the best,' Edward said not wanting to jump to any conclusions for Mary's sake.

The story was changing fast and he kept thinking what was best for his brother. A brother he would never see again. Howarth interrupted his thoughts.

'I'm sending some of my officers in the morning and I will be coming to the Hall as soon as possible tomorrow. At

141

this moment in time I do need to tell you to inform your sister in law and niece that in no circumstance are they to leave Whitby and the same rule applies to Albert Smithers, is that clear?' Howarth stressed. 'I need to know the whereabouts of everyone who lives and works at the Hall.'

'Perfectly, I'll let Bella know in the morning and I'll personally make sure that I see Mary and Albert to tell them, they live in the Lodge which is just on the outskirts of the estate,' said Edward hesitating. 'What about James Smithers, anything Albert is up to, his father will be more than a part of?'

'You leave that to me, remember no one leaves Whitby, including yourself Mr. Green, is that clear?'

'Yes perfectly.'

# Chapter 18

Edward closed the door of the room, his head swimming full of thoughts about what exactly had happened to David. One of the theories he had thought of was that someone had been paid by James and Albert Smithers to kill David and had attempted to murder Jimmy, but it was difficult to decide just how involved Bella was in all this terrible business. It was a thought that was too dreadful to think about just now. Howarth was right when he had told him that he had no place in this twisted tale and it was really a matter for the police and yet somehow Edward felt more than anything he had to protect his niece.

Edward looked outside, he could see from the windows of the main hall that the light at the end of the courtyard was still not visible which told him that the fog still had not cleared yet. Tired from his phone call with Howarth, he headed towards the main staircase and was surprised to see Betty there. Edward thought that it wasn't just a coincidence that she was there alone at this time of night and he knew instantly she had been waiting to speak to him. He didn't know Betty that well but knew from his brother that she had worked for him for many years and was a trusted member of the household.

She looked worried and still wore her uniform even though it was well past her working hours.

'Sir, if I may be so bold, could I have a quiet word with you?' she said uneasily and stepped forward to be nearer to Edward.

'Yes, of course whatever is it that keeps you up so late at night Betty?' Edward asked aware of the importance of what she might tell him and hoped it could shed some light on what exactly was going on.

'There's been some strange comings and goings of late in the Hall and I've tried to tell Bella, er sorry Sir, Mrs.

Green but she's not been herself which of course is quite understandable given the circumstances.'

Betty sounded as though she was about to cry and produced a handkerchief from her pocket.

'I think between you and me that Bella's had a lot on her mind before any of this terrible tragedy ever began. I know it's really none of my business but I've got to tell someone, you see it's ever since James got involved in the family which must be a couple of years ago. They've been coming up here for a long time.'

'Oh,' Edward said unaware of the extent of the friendship between his brother and Smithers' family. 'I'd no idea they were all such good friends, I know James and David knew each other but...'

'Not so much David but Bella...They're bad news if you ask me but I know it's not my place and up until now I've respected Mr. Green's opinion and kept quiet but now though I wished I hadn't. You see the thing is, if I'd said something earlier then maybe Mr. Green could still be alive.'

Suddenly one of the bedroom doors opened from the corridor above them. A figure appeared at the top of the stairs and Edward couldn't quite make out who it was, whoever it was seemed quite tall so he was taken aback when he heard Bella's voice, who was herself a petite woman.

'It's you Edward and Betty, thank goodness. I couldn't sleep and heard voices,' Bella whispered and started to come down the stairs. 'Since David has gone, it's been very tough to sleep and sometimes...' She wiped her eyes. 'Well it's difficult and I have these terrible nightmares.'

'You've been through such a lot my dear Bella,' Betty said taking hold of Bella's arm and leading her back upstairs. 'I'll bring you a nice cup of cocoa but firstly you need your sleep.'

'Thank you, Betty,' Bella said while nodding a goodnight to Edward. 'You've been so good to me over the years Betty, what would I do without you?'

Edward waited a few minutes and considered whether to wait for Betty after she had helped Bella. He already felt exhausted however and now had the odious task of telling Bella that the police suspected foul play so he decided that whatever Betty was going to tell him, it could wait until the morning. He looked at his watch, it had just gone midnight, morning now didn't seem so far away after all.

Edward woke later than he wanted. The sun was out already streaming through his windows suggesting it was at least mid morning. It was the second morning Edward had simply overslept. He was annoyed with himself as he had wanted to wake earlier to find both Betty and Bella but guessed the combination of both the sea air and the shock of David's death had taken its toll.

Looking out of the curtains in his room, he could see bright sunshine. The fog of his first night had completely disappeared and there was now a strong sea breeze which was blowing the garden leaves scattering them around the lawn at the front of the house. It was then that he noticed two police cars parked on the main driveway and presumed they had arrived to tell Bella about the poison that had actually killed David rather than the suspected heart attack which was named the initial cause of death.

He quickly dressed and entered the room where to his surprise Mary, Albert and Bella were seated with three senior looking police officers.

'I take it you're Edward Green, Detective Inspector Dudley,' the Inspector shook his hand. 'Detective Superintendent Howarth is at this very moment travelling here and will join us later.'

Dudley gestured for Edward to take a seat. Edward was surprised that there were three officers and presumed it was due to the fact that David was after all, a man with a great deal of power in this area and if this was a murder as Howarth had said on the phone, then that was something that would be taken very seriously.

'I'm afraid I have bad news which has been most unexpected, as this case has sadly taken a rather nasty turn over night. It would seem in light of the new evidence, we have now subsequently been informed and updated into what would seem the exact nature of Mr Green's death. We now know he died from poisoning entering the blood stream. Unfortunately, I'm afraid to inform everybody that we are now dealing with not just one murder but a double murder on our hands,' Dudley said removing his hat and coat and placing them on a nearby chair.

A silence ensured which gave Dudley an opportunity to look carefully around the room. Edward didn't look at the others but he was aghast to hear the news that somehow during the night there had been yet another death. He suddenly thought about Jimmy. A dreadful thought went through Edward's mind, had Jimmy taken a turn for the worst in the night or was his imagination running away with him and telling him that someone had finished the job off and killed his good friend.

'But I don't understand, Jimmy was recovering well so I was led to believe, in fact I saw him just last night. I was under the impression that he would be fine?' Edward asked wondering how George had taken the news. This was a bitter blow for Edward, first his brother and now Jimmy.

'No Mr. Green, you're mistaken, it is not Jimmy but it is the lady who works as the Head Cook Betty. I'm sorry to inform you but last night she was found dead lying on the kitchen floor with a knife stuck in her back. It would seem that whoever killed her, did so by puncturing her lungs so hard she was dead within seconds.

The kitchen staff that found her reported the death straight away and as we got here in the early hours of this morning it would seem she'd been killed at least a few hours earlier, the time of death was probably just after midnight. A nasty callous death by all accounts, although from the evidence gathered so far, it seems she put up a bit of a struggle but the fact she was caught unawares gave the murderer the vital element of surprise which as you all know is essential for all good killers.

The fact that it appears there was no sign of any forced entry to the Hall leaves us or rather me in the rather delicate position of treating you all as suspects. I don't quite have an angle on things yet but believe you me I'm about to. Nobody including any members of staff will leave the house unless for provisions escorted by a police officer which I will post this afternoon. This whole house is a scene of two crimes and everyone is now a suspect.'

'But,' said Mary who was obviously still in shock. 'How can that be, I don't understand, apart from staff, we are a family and everyone loved dear daddy?' she started to cry. 'Why on earth would they want to hurt him, he did a lot of good for this village and I can't think of anyone that would do this to him and as for dear darling Betty, she wouldn't hurt a fly?'

'Ha, that's where you're quite mistaken your father was very much liked but there is obviously someone that thought your father was better off to them dead than still being here.'

Mary shook her head. 'And Betty, surely no one would want to kill her, this is quite ridiculous, first my father and now Betty, why it could be any one of us next.'

'That indeed may be the case, so that's why you are all better here under police supervision,' Dudley said nonchalantly.

'I say old chap,' it was the first time Albert had spoken and he seemed agitated. 'You mean to say somebody would kill David and Betty and what's this about some man called Jimmy?'

'I will of course assure everyone that we shall question each and every one of you and you'll all be able to tell us your thoughts and opinions when it's your turn,' Dudley said firmly. 'But all in good time.'

'I can't believe any of this,' Mary said sobbing choking back tears.

'Although it may be difficult I would ask for everyone to more or less go about their everyday business and we will be hopefully interviewing you all today.'

Dudley took out his notebook from an old tattered briefcase. 'By the way Mr. Smithers,' Dudley said. 'I've allocated more time to interview yourself, there's some other business that we need to discuss relating to something which you will find of interest,' Dudley explained as he turned to look at Albert.

Albert was just about to say something in his defence when the door swung open. Jimmy Roberts entered catching Mary's eye.

'Dudley.' Jimmy nodded

'Inspector Roberts.' Dudley smiled it was obvious the two men had been previously acquainted.

'Inspector Roberts has been a great help to me and has explained one or two matters.'

Albert shifted uncomfortably in his chair and even Mary looked anxious.

'Yes we are very fortunate to have Roberts with us and he certainly will be helping.'

'Look here. I don't know exactly what these shenanigans are about,' Albert said abruptly standing to his feet. 'I've had absolutely no dealings with Green or Betty, there's no connection whatsoever. You can dig as much as you want but you won't find anything on me, the only link I have with Green is that I have married his daughter, whom I dearly love.'

'I'm quite sure you do,' Dudley said sarcastically. He was in charge and that's the way things were going to be round here. He'd met these posh folks before and they certainly wouldn't be intimidating him. His round spectacles were slightly steamed by now and he took them off to wipe with a cloth he kept in his top pocket.

'I'm afraid you're barking up the wrong tree,' Albert smiled as he spoke.

Albert's arrogance told Edward that even if he was involved, it may prove to be a pointless waste of police time by trying to do any real delving into the case, as nothing may be found after all. Albert and his father were far too slippery characters for that.

From listening to Dudley, Edward couldn't help but think about the time of Betty's death. Dudley had been quite specific that she'd died just after midnight. Edward recalled looking at the clock last night when Betty was called away by Bella and the clock had said the same time. It surely couldn't be a coincidence that Betty was just about to tell him something that was on her mind. That left Edward thinking about Bella or more to the point her involvement if any.

Edward had to admit to himself that the business of the diamonds seemed almost a side show to the two deaths that had happened. He thought back to Betty trying to warn him and wished he had found time to listen to her last night.

He also started to think that if Albert was involved then perhaps he himself was now was a sitting duck. Suddenly he regretted coming back up to Yorkshire, Howarth was right all along, this was a police matter and now he was virtually a prisoner in Herron Hall unable to leave until an investigation had taken place and what may or could happen by that time was a very worrying thought.

Edward knew as he stood there that things were about to take a turn for the worse and right now the only person that he could think that could help them was Jimmy. He realised that right now he was liaising with Dudley and so he would have to wait patiently until an opportune time presented itself.

The day seemed to drag and Mary didn't help matters by periodically crying and chastising herself for not being there to support her father. It aggrieved Edward to witness her so distraught but there was nothing he could do only to tell Jimmy exactly what he knew so far. He'd already informed him about the fake suicide letter that Bella had showed him. There was also Betty's warning last night which had been suddenly interrupted by Bella. After that coincidentally Betty had been murdered in the most evil of circumstances.

Edward tried to remain practical and think about all the facts he had so far. The more he thought about matters though he could only conclude that everything seemed to point to Albert Smithers who luckily was at this very moment being questioned by the police. His absence from the room felt a relief and Edward turned his attentions to Bella who throughout this morning had been very quiet.

His sister in law was a very private person and Edward imagined that all the upset had taken its toll on Bella and now with the death of Betty who had been a family friend, seemed a cruel blow. It appeared that the stress of events was beginning to take a terrible strain on Bella. Yet in his own mind, Bella seemed a complex character and he remained unsure about her motives last night with Betty.

'The police are going to want to know everything Bella, is there anything else that you think they ought to know? ' Edward asked trying to help his sister in law.

'No, there's nothing else Edward, I still can't believe David is dead and now Betty,' Bella sighed. 'It's too much for us to take.'

'Yes, I know hopefully, we will just have to let the police do their job and besides...' Edward gestured to Mary who was sitting near the window with her back turned to them. 'I still think both James and Albert may still be incriminated,' Edward said whispering out of ear shot of Mary.

'I don't know about that, by the way how long do you think the interviews will take?' Bella asked trying to change the subject by looking at her watch which already showed half past eleven and though food was the last thing on her mind she was aware the kitchen staff would be preparing lunch.

'I think this could be a long day,' Edward hesitated as he could hear footsteps from the corridor and a familiar voice with a strong cockney accent.

'Good morning, please don't stand on my behalf. I'd like to introduce myself, the name's Detective Superintendent Howarth, I've already acquainted myself with the Green family. I'm here to take over this enquiry and I'm sure Detective Inspector Dudley and with the help of Inspector Roberts have done a tremendous job but I'll be in charge now.'

Howarth nodded to Dudley and Jimmy. 'Thank you but ...well, I'll be taking things from here and I hope for everybody's sake to conclude matters very soon.'

Howarth lifted his heavy looking briefcase onto the table and looked towards Edward.

'Well in that case, I believe that the interviews are being in conducted in the library, shall we go through?'

Edward nodded but felt rather puzzled by Howarth's rather sudden appearance. When he'd spoken to Howarth yesterday morning, he'd been quite specific about telling Edward that he would be taking the train up to Hull this very morning. The first train as Edward knew didn't depart from Kings Cross until 6.30. Edward checked his watch again just to make sure he'd not lost a large chunk of the day by oversleeping, his watch confirmed that it was just before midday. How then he thought to himself had Howarth managed to get here so fast. Howarth, who was naturally an observant man must have read Edward's thoughts.

'Brought the car last night, very bad fog all the way from London.'

Edward knew this wasn't true from having talked to a member of staff who had returned to the Hall last night. John had told him that even at Hull station it had been a clear night as he had observed how bright the stars were, feeling pleased with himself that he'd spotted Orion in the summer sky. In fact, as he thought on, John had mentioned that it wasn't until near Whitby station that the fog had come down which was often the case if there was a change in temperature as hot and cold air formed out at sea and blew the sea mist in land.

The thought puzzled Edward but as there seemed no mileage for Howarth to lie, he felt it more important to put his mind to concentrate on Howarth's questioning which even as a trained solicitor knew would be tricky, though in some ways he was there only as bystander. Still he felt an obligation to David to try and make sure the investigation was conducted properly.

The library was a large ornate room filled with first copies of impressive titles. Edward knew it was David's favourite room in the house. Edward felt such a sense of loss it was quite overwhelming.

'Right,' Howarth shut the door behind him and Edward was surprised to see he was by himself. 'We'll make this short and sweet, is there anything that I need to know?'

Howarth's direct manner didn't surprise Edward, men of the law generally were blunt with few pleasantries in conversation and no matter how the interviewee answered and put their point of view forwards it was pointless as men of the law only heard key words. Edward knew this was standard practice and was nothing personal.

'There was nothing really out of the ordinary,' Edward said. 'Well... except the house keeper Betty Wilson, poor old girl tried to tell me something last night. In fact, I think she'd stayed up specially to do so.'

'And did she?'

'No, that's just the thing, she was about to say something and seemed quite upset as to what it was but Bella came out of a room upstairs. This might sound ridiculous but it was as though she wanted to stop Betty from telling me some information. After that Betty headed towards the kitchen to make some hot cocoa. I could kick myself now as I should have stayed up after that and found Betty to talk to but naturally I thought I'd see her in the morning when I didn't feel so tired but obviously I never had the chance,' said Edward still feeling annoyed with himself.

It was only now that he realised she'd stayed up specially to tell him something and now whatever it was would never be known.

'I guess you could say that she took that information to her grave,' Howarth remarked.

'Yes.'

'Well, we'll never know now I'm afraid,' Howarth said and then put his pen down. 'There's no point to think about such matters. You will be pleased to know that you do not need to stay any longer than needed. I can't however be seen to let you leave Whitby for a few days but you're free to come and go from the house as you see fit.'

'Right, I'll make a telephone call to my wife and let her know,' Edward felt relieved as he spoke.

As Edward closed the door he saw that Bella was standing further down the corridor. It looked like she was next to be questioned or perhaps she'd been eavesdropping, Edward couldn't be sure. Edward hoped for her sake and Mary's that she would be strong enough to undergo the rather forthright questioning of the formidable Detective Howarth. He wished he could stay with her but knew even asking Howarth was a fruitless task.

Bella wasn't present for lunch and Edward found himself sitting with Albert who remained silent throughout the meal. Mary had slipped into a quiet mood but periodically kept repeating that her father had been murdered and that somehow there had been a dreadful mistake of identity and she must try and help. She concluded by saying Betty had been a victim of some sort of robbery that had gone dreadfully wrong.

Edward looked closely at Mary and realised for the first time that she looked incredibly young to Edward and quite innocent from the girls he had known in London, far too young and innocent for the likes of Albert Smithers he thought to himself. After lunch there was still no sign of Bella so Edward decided to try and talk to Jimmy. He'd tried all day to find him but luck was on his side.

'Jimmy, what's happening?' Edward asked relieved at last to get some answers.

'Inspector Dudley is a good sort and is concerned for Mary. Two murders in a short space of a few weeks does not bode well. I'm also worried, Mary needs to be careful.'

'I know. Do you think she is safe?'

'I've asked Dudley to appoint a police officer just to keep an extra eye on her.'

'The suicide note was fake, I know that for sure. The question is wouldn't Bella know that too?'

'It's strange. My father says she's not been herself for a while now. She's kept herself away from the staff more and more not that she ever been that friendly.'

'Well, let's just keep alert and Jimmy.'

'Yes.'

'Watch your back.'

# Chapter 19

Edward sat with his hands in his head, feeling helpless. So many things had happened. The attempt on Jimmy's life a few weeks back, David and now Betty. He wanted to go and confront Albert but he knew it would never do any good. He knew David would have said to him, lie low and wait and the truth will come to you but suddenly Herron Hall was a place that he wanted to escape from but he knew the reality was at least for a few more days he would be here as a prisoner.

It was late afternoon when Bella emerged from the make shift interview room in the library and she looked absolutely exhausted. Edward was still confused by the fake suicide letter and knew Jimmy thought the same. Deep in thought he was surprised to find Bella outside in the courtyard.

'Are you alright Bella?' Edward asked accurately aware of the awkwardness between them.

'I think Howarth would arrest Albert right now as well as his father James who also is being interviewed down in Sussex but there's not enough evidence to go on. The fact that Betty was murdered and David cannot he ignored though,' Bella explained thoughtfully.

'And the attempt on Jimmy's life?'

'There could have been three lives lost in this sordid business, it was just luck on Jimmy's part to be alive.'

As Edward said the words out loud it felt too raw and painful.

'That's right but two deaths, is too much my dear Edward. Too much,' Bella said pushing her hair nervously to one side as she spoke.

Dinner was a sombre occasion that night and strained to say the least with Bella, Mary, Albert and Edward. Thankfully Jimmy joined them which made the conversation a little easier. Edward observed how pleased

Mary was for Jimmy's unexpected company. It wasn't wasted on Jimmy either who seemed only to happy to be with her.

For Bella and Mary's sake Edward tried to steer the conversation away from anything to do with the investigation but in fairness to everyone, there seemed little else to talk about so thankfully, dinner was quickly over and eventually Mary, Albert and Jimmy excused themselves leaving Bella and Edward alone.

Edward felt rather tired and Bella soon said she wanted to go to bed herself as she had a rather bad headache. Edward was relieved as this meant he could just sit by the French doors in the dining room and be by himself to think. Once the table was cleared and he'd made small talk with the servants, he settled himself down, pouring a neat scotch from the decanter which was left on a tray in the room.

Edward was missing something and he suddenly felt like a pawn in a very clever chess game that he couldn't control. He kept coming back to David and Betty's death. Edward sipped his drink, his mind was in overtime but the night air had a nasty chill which thankfully kept his mind sharp. He thought back to when he'd first told Jimmy about Albert Smithers in the Stag Pub in London. Jimmy, knew more than he was letting on. He looked at his pocket watch, he needed to see Jimmy. Just as he was finishing the last sips of his drink, the very person he wanted to see also wanted to see him.

'What are you not telling me?' Edward said whilst gesturing for Jimmy to close the door.

'You know this is police business.'

'Jimmy I need to know, my brother is dead.'

'Alright but this for now goes no further. You know I'm not officially part of this case. Well, I took it upon myself to do... shall we say some digging around.'

'And?'

'A few months ago, I was assigned to a case, a big one I might add. Whilst I was interviewing a witness, both James and Albert Smithers' names came about in the conversation.

He said they'd been directly involved with illegal dealings connected to Amsterdam and Amsterdam as we know is a city synonymous for diamonds and the dirtier side of things, smuggling them.'

'Have you told Howarth?'

'He is fully aware but so far hasn't made any arrests as he knows there is no substantial evidence only speculation.'

'I wish he'd hurry things up,' Edward said impatiently. 'The law is frustrating you know that.'

'I feel things are going to take a turn for the worse.'

'Or maybe for the better, in fairness Edward nothing untoward is going to happen whilst Howarth is here. He'll watch things like a hawk,' Jimmy looked at his watch. 'Sorry I've got to rush but I'd better go, I've got to meet with Howarth. Come on chin up.'

Edward sat alone trying hard to get comfortable in the armchair which seemed impossible. He felt very sad but he knew he must try make things better. After an hour or so deep in concentration he slowly started to put all the missing pieces and details together that had bothered him of late. Perhaps he thought to himself Jimmy was over his head. Two murders had taken place and although both Jimmy and Howarth were now at the Hall, it didn't give Edward any reassurance; who would be next he thought to himself.

His train of thoughts were leading him to think something that was unthinkable, the realisation that danger was not far away. Suddenly he heard voices from upstairs and recognised one of them to be Bella's but couldn't quite make out who the male voice was.

Edward listened but the voices had once more become distant. Intrigued, he crept out of the room and up the side stairs that doubled back and led onto the main hallway. He knew this because the twins had played hide and seek whilst visiting for the wedding. He slowly crept up the stairs keeping low to the wall in case he cast a shadow.

'This has got way out of hand Bella,' the voice was Albert's. 'I was just supposed to marry your daughter and kill David which would look like suicide. We now thanks to you, have two murders on our hands, David and Betty, two people who were well liked.'

'I know, the situation seems intolerable but what can we do?'

'There are far too many loose ends. It's Jimmy who worries me, I'm afraid he'll have to go, it's just poor luck he's here,' Albert said his voice now getting louder.

'Do you think Jimmy suspects Howarth's involvement in all this? I reckon Jimmy may be on to us and could know about Howarth.'

'Yes Howarth has surprised me somewhat. It was rather foolish of him and I must say out of character to send some amateurs to try to kill Jimmy. It seems however Jimmy was quicker with his gun as he managed to shoot them first before they shot him. They died but as we know Jimmy unfortunately has survived but before they died I just hope they didn't talk to him about my involvement.'

'I doubt that but we have underestimated Jimmy, it seems he is cleverer than we thought. I'm afraid we'll just have to hope things will work out to our advantage,' Bella said her voice faltering slightly.

Albert got to his feet, he was angry about Betty's death which he saw as unnecessary and blamed Bella. Another death cast more suspicion something which he wanted to avoid. He was not about to let Bella off the hook so easily.

'And let's not forget it's your fault entirely that Edward was not duped into believing the suicide note, how could you forget that David was left handed. I call that a school boy error.'

'Howarth's men should have finished Jimmy off. If anything has been said then it has nothing to do with me,' Bella retorted.

She moved closer to the door allowing Edward to get a good look at his sister in law which made him dislike her in a way he never thought possible. 'They should have finished Jimmy off in hospital. It's your snooping brother in law Edward, he's too nosy, he makes me nervous, do keep an eye on him.'

Edward couldn't believe what he was hearing and had to stop himself from shouting out in shock. So, he was right, it was Bella, along with Albert and who could have thought Howarth. This was a surprise. It shocked Edward, Howarth was a Superintendent, it made Edward think just what other things he may be involved in.

Edward remembered Howarth's telephone call and his insistence to find information about David and to be in charge of this case. He'd told him that he had a personal interest. Thinking back to Howarth's arrival to the Hall, it had been impossible for him to arrive so quickly and he had lied about the weather being foggy when in fact the fog had cleared around Hull and only the last part of his journey had been foggy.

Edward's mind raced ahead. This whole hideous plan had to be about money. His brother was an incredibly wealthy man, it seemed his money had been too much of a temptation. Edward's head felt warm as he stood and he lay it against the cold of the wall to make him hopefully think clearer.

The door swung open and Bella came out of the room rearranging her collar quickly. It seemed however the conversation was not quite over.

'Your personal involvement with Howarth has deceived you. You're not thinking clearly,' Albert said.

'Like all relationships it's complicated, you of all people should know that,' Bella said.

Edward was surprised to hear this. Perhaps the reason for David's death was not just financial, if what he'd just heard was true then it would seem that his sister in law had been in love with Howarth. To kill David made perfect sense and the money from his death was just a bonus to the crime.

The room fell silent for a few minutes and Edward thought this was a good opportunity to sneak away but he heard a third voice from inside the room and stepped closer again, he didn't recognise the voice.

'You two had better get your act together.'

There was a strange accent to the voice which Edward couldn't recognise. 'You're forgetting my dearest Albert that this fine mess we have found ourselves in is down to you. It's your doing for going bankrupt in the first place.'

Edward shuffled back to where he had been stood but still couldn't make out who the person was.

'You married me,' Albert shot back. 'And let's face it, the marriage only came about because you thought I had money. It serves you right when you found out that I'm completely broke, that's why you're in this mess, greed, sheer and utter greed.'

The woman now had come into view and Edward could plainly see that she was strikingly beautiful, far more than Mary. She was tall, graceful and had blue piercing eyes with long auburn hair that fell down her back.

'Now you're married to her, I suppose she's made you have doubts but you know the deal, you've got to still kill her or there's no money for any of us,' the woman said.

'Elizabeth, only two people were going to get hurt in all this and now as I've already pointed out, it seems we've already got two deaths and still our dearest Mary is well and truly still alive. Unless she's killed soon you're right, there's no money,' Albert said coldly.

The woman, Elizabeth must be Albert's wife, this story was unraveling at speed, Edward thought to himself.

'I agree with Albert, this whole affair has got way out of hand,' Bella said shaking her head and directed her speech towards the woman. 'The thing is Elizabeth we should have never involved Edward, by David's brother visiting the Hall along with Jimmy, it only made trouble for us. I'm afraid we've complicated the game somewhat. We needed Jimmy to die. He's asked too many questions,' Bella said.

'We had to kill David and it's a pity that Howarth wasn't able to bribe the pathologist. I felt confident he would go along with the suicide story.'

'The thing is, what do we do now?' Albert asked impatient, not wanting to hear the answer.

Elizabeth walked forwards looking Albert right in the eye. 'We get rid of Mary like we should have in the first place, instead of this flimsy plan.'

'We need to be patient and wait at least for a while until Howarth can calm things down here,' Albert reasoned. 'You've always said he'd square things off so why not let him do his job.'

'No, I agree with Elizabeth, we get rid of that daughter of mine once and for all.'

'That's the best news I've heard mother and then I can remarry you and all Mary's wealth will be kept together.'

What Edward was hearing was unbelievable in fact so much so that he had to steady himself. That was the thing about life until you really know someone you never really know them. In fairness he'd never properly known his sister in law before she'd married David. He'd always had suspicions that she'd married him for his wealth. Although Bella was born from aristocracy, Edward had on more than one occasion suspected that her family had not left their inheritance to her.

He'd never liked her from David's first introduction but optimistically assumed that the marriage was to all intent and purposes bearable. This was news that truly shocked him. Bella being Howarth's lover and having another child who appeared little older than Mary herself. He wondered if David had known any of this sorry tale before he married Bella. He recalled David telling him that Bella had gone to an art school in Switzerland a couple of years before she met him, in fact that was probably the time she'd most likely to have given birth to Elizabeth which Edward presumed was born out of wedlock.

Elizabeth must have been brought up somewhere and then Bella had gone on to marry David. He'd always wondered why they didn't start a family straight away and only had Mary perhaps now he knew the reason. Bella had never seemed very affectionate to Mary but Edward had reasoned this was just Bella's nature. She always had a coldness from as long as he'd known her but Edward never thought she could be capable of such a despicable act of cruelty which was now deemed as horrific acts of murder.

He still couldn't believe she'd murdered her husband with a devious plan to allow David's money to be left to Mary. Then the attempt on Jimmy's life to prevent him obtaining information about smuggling diamonds.

Lastly poor Betty who just happened to have suspicions about David's death and now Edward would never know if Betty knew any of this terrible story. Edward guessed that she may have known quite a bit of it and because of that she had paid the ultimate price.

'I've just about had enough of this,' Elizabeth said coldly. 'Where is Howarth?'

'He'll be tying things up downstairs and then he's staying at the local tavern just outside the village,' Bella said.

Elizabeth went in her bag and took out a small pistol. 'I'm going to finish this once and for all, we need to get rid of Mary, when she's gone everything is yours Albert and then ours.'

'You mean all yours,' Albert said bitterly. He looked as though he was having cold feet about the whole thing and Edward wondered if deep down he actually cared more for Mary than the callous woman that he regarded as his real wife.

'We had a good thing going with the diamonds and then with Mary and David gone all this... we...we just need to be careful. Once the heat goes away, it will all be how it should,' Bella said trying to keep things calm.

Elizabeth put her arm through Albert's but Edward noticed he didn't do the same. Suddenly Elizabeth was heading to the door. Edward had no choice but to run to the next door along the corridor which was another of the guest bedrooms which luckily was empty. He needed to think quickly, if he'd heard correctly, they were just about to kill Mary. Surely, they wouldn't get away with it but who knows.

Edward left the door ajar just enough so he could see but not be seen. Elizabeth had put the pistol back in her bag and now was heading off to the Lodge where Mary would be. He knew that somehow, he had to warn her. Naturally he would have gone straight to the police but he'd have to get past Howarth. Dudley was in Whitby and there was no way of getting in touch with him without Howarth knowing.

He couldn't just stand there and do nothing knowing that his niece was the next victim, he had to find Jimmy. Edward was a tall strong man but he was no match for Elizabeth with her pistol. A couple of minutes had already gone and Edward knew he had to be quick. Right now, the only advantage Edward had is they didn't know he knew their plan, which meant they wouldn't be expecting him.

Being as quiet as he could, he crept into the main part of the house and headed to Jimmy's room. If he wasn't there he would have no other means of help. He hadn't time to inform the staff and he was now aware he may not be able to trust them.

Some of the staff may be part of this twisted plan. It was a thought that he pushed to the back of his mind. It was a journey of only a few minutes but it seemed to last forever. Jimmy's door was shut so Edward knocked loudly. There was no reply. There was no time for niceties, he pushed the door as hard as he could.

Jimmy's body was slumped on the floor in front of a chest of drawers. Edward lifted his body, he'd sustained a heavy blow to his head showing congealed blood that had trickled down his face. He'd been knocked unconscious. Edward checked his pulse, he was still alive and although Jimmy looked terrible, Edward felt confident his condition was not life threatening but that seemed little comfort to Edward. Jimmy was little use to him in this state and more importantly he would not be able to help Mary.

A cold feeling of fear seeped into Edward's body. He was on his own. It was a sombre thought and he knew that time was not on his side.

Edward had led a charmed life but as a solicitor when he was in court defending justice he had a strength that had often surprised himself over the years. Though it was not a physical strength it was a mental determination that had won him many a case and had made him the fine solicitor he was.

He clenched his fists in an act of defiance more to show himself his courage. He looked back at Jimmy, he would be alright. He probably would come round naturally. Knowing his friend was safe he headed down the corridor.

If he could just get to the Lodge before Elizabeth did, he may just have a chance of getting Mary away but as Elizabeth had already had a slight head start it seemed rather unlikely.

He then remembered a short cut that led to the Lodge which was actually at the back of the Hall. Earlier in the year, he'd played hide and seek there with the twins and had noticed a narrow path that ran alongside the main house. He doubted Elizabeth even knew about it and if he could run quickly, he might be able to get there to warn Mary. He quietly crept down the stairs and just as he left the Hall, he took a letter opener that he'd noticed earlier which had been left by the window near the main entrance. It wasn't much of a weapon when facing a pistol but somehow it made him feel braver. He tucked it up his sleeve hoping he wouldn't need to use it.

He opened the side door of the house and made his way round the bottom windows of the back parlour. Thankfully there was no one around and he quickly was able to get to the orangery where the path started. As the summer had been particularly warm the garden looked different from a few weeks earlier when he'd visited with Verity. The shrubbery seemed to have grown and at first he couldn't see the path at all. Minutes passed but Edward still couldn't find the tiny cobbles. Soon it became obvious the path had been taken over by hydrangea bushes. In one last desperate attempt Edward pushed the bushes aside revealing at last the small narrow path.

Edward admitted to himself he was scared but couldn't help but smile. Life seemed ironic. A few weeks ago, he'd been here as a guest for Mary and Albert's wedding, he'd had his suspicions about Albert Smithers but a few weeks on, he was now running through over grown bushes to save Mary's life with nothing more than a letter opener for protection. He'd now found out that his sister in law had an illegitimate child called Elizabeth. He'd no real idea as to who the father was perhaps Elizabeth had been Howarth's all along. It was impossible to know if they'd always been together but from what he'd just overheard anything seemed believable.

The sky had turned quite grey signalling a storm may be coming. Edward ran along the path and soon could feel raindrops staring to hit the ground. In some ways this acted as a means to cool him down and made his mind more alert. As he turned the corner he could see the Lodge which was situated at the edge of some woods. There was no sign of Elizabeth but this didn't mean she wasn't here as she could already have entered the house. With any luck Mary might not be at home but his heart sunk as he could hear piano music coming from the house which confirmed Mary's presence.

Edward was in touching distance of the Lodge and checked the front door was closed. He doubted that Elizabeth would enter and close the door and this gave him hope that he'd arrived first.

Mary had spent all morning feeling anxious. She was devastated by her father's death and now the police had confirmed her father had been murdered she had felt helpless. She instinctively guessed it was Albert and his father James but knew better than to share her suspicions. She felt alone and afraid and hoped that she was not in any way to blame.

She had known when she married Albert that her father had been careful to only give her a small share of his wealth. He'd told her that he'd done this to protect her finances. Now that her father was dead this had left a terrible conundrum as what to do next. She had overnight become the sole beneficiary of her father's estate. Even she had been surprised by her father's wealth and that she and not her mother had inherited the whole lot.

Mary's problem was that all her wealth had now become her husband's and this was a thought that had caused her to have sleepless nights and one that she wished she wasn't in the pickle with which she now found herself.

To confront Albert about money would be foolish and she hoped that somehow the police could find enough evidence to put her husband away for a very long time but in many ways, she knew this to be unlikely from what she had already learnt in the few weeks of really knowing her husband.

Albert was as slippery as an eel. She had quickly worked out that he hadn't a half pence coin to put together. The facade of wealth had been elaborately put together and the truth was far worse than she ever thought. The Smithers' family had declared bankruptcy several years ago but luckily for them had lived on the goodwill of an elderly aunt.

As they were not beneficiaries of her will, they lived in hope that she would reach a grand old age. It appeared that while ever she was alive, there was just enough money to allow them to live in relative comfort.

Mary had so many questions which her mother seemed to evade which only led her to feel more isolated and confused. She really needed to confide in someone but when she relayed her fears to Detective Howarth, it had been a fruitless task and she felt that she had not been taken seriously.

Mary's fingers hit the notes and the melodic sound echoed from the hallway so much so that she didn't see Edward enter and she would have been even more alarmed if she'd have seen the fear in his eyes or the letter opener which on entering the house, he had pointed in front of him acting as his only means of defence.

'Mary, thank god it's you, are you on your own?' Edward said trying to sound much calmer than he felt inwardly.

'Yes, whatever is the matter, what's wrong Edward?' Mary said immediately becoming scared, she'd felt uneasy for days and now Edward was here, it only confirmed her fears.

'I've not much time to explain but you've got to get out of here, this Lodge, the Hall and I mean now Mary,' Edward stressed wanting to get them away as soon as possible. 'We've absolutely no time to lose.'

'You're scaring me Edward,' Mary said her voice was very quiet.

Edward's eyes darted around the room checking that nobody had entered the Lodge, he needed more than ever to be alert and listened carefully to see if Elizabeth was now here.

'Mary, I don't want to panic you but go now and get your coat, we have to go.'

'Wait here,' she said trying to remain calm.

'You need to be quick, we've got to hurry,' Edward said anxiously trying to help Mary gather a few belongings. 'We are in real danger.'

Mary looked up and could see Edward was frightened. She didn't quite understand what exactly was going on but presumed it had something to do with Albert.

'Is it Albert?' she asked not wanting to know the answer but in some ways, she always knew that the inevitable would happen and she would be in danger from him.

'Yes, but if we hang around, I daren't think of the consequences Mary, we have to hurry your life could be in real danger,'

'Is it that serious?' Mary asked hardly daring to hear the truth.

'Yes,' Edward answered firmly. 'I'll explain everything that I know on the way.'

Mary quickly ran to the cloakroom to get her shoes but Edward knew when he heard her scream that it was too late,

Elizabeth was now here. Edward also knew the last thing in the world was to make any sudden movement and he stood still weighing up his options.

There was always the possibility that Elizabeth didn't know he was here, after all they'd talked quietly and the cloakroom was a good distance away from where they'd been standing in the hallway. He needed that to be the case as the element of surprise was his only hope.

He crept quietly to the far side of the hall and could clearly see Elizabeth holding a gun to Mary's head. Mary stood motionless gripped by fear and unable to move. For what seemed minutes with only the clock for noise, time elapsed and both women stood motionless without a sound between them.

Edward wondered now knowing the story himself, if Mary knew she was looking at her half sister who although at first glance looked nothing like her after seeing them both together they were however far more similar than Edward had first realised. The difference between the two women was that Elizabeth's face wore hate and bitterness but Mary for all her somewhat spoilt prissiness was a good kind person.

Edward could see that if he crept back outside he then could come in from the front of the house and that would allow him to be exactly behind Elizabeth. It was a risky plan and he didn't want to take his eyes away from Mary for a second but if he was to do anything at all, it was his only chance.

He took his shoes off as to make no noise and slipped out the door. The sun had now come out and shone directly on the window panes causing the brightness of the glass to distort Edward's view for a second. It was then in that momentarily lapse of concentration that he felt a sharp penetrating blow to his head and for a few seconds he felt that he was going to fall backwards. He stumbled and tried to regain his balance not sure of what was happening. His head felt like it had been sliced in half and the pain seemed unbearable, he could only hold his head with both hands to try and take the throbbing away.

Somehow after swaying for a couple of seconds, he managed to regain his balance. He looked around confused as to who had managed to hit him so hard. He felt sure the blow couldn't have come from Elizabeth as she was standing near the cloakroom and besides she couldn't possibly have that amount of strength. As his vision started to become clearer, he saw that the blow had come from Albert. He must have followed him down the path and waited for an opportunity to strike him down.

With all the strength he could muster, Edward charged forwards and managed to knock Albert clean off his feet, his body thudding on the floor and the heavy metal bar that was in his hands thankfully rolled to the side.

Albert however it seemed was not going to give up that easy and soon got back on his feet and subsequently punched Edward hitting him square on with Edward taking a hard blow to his right cheek.

Adrenaline kicked in and before Edward knew it instincts had made him give a hard kick to Albert's knee cap causing him to whine out loud and double up in pain. Edward's heart raced as he knew he had now got the better of him and kicked him again hard in the back of the head.

Albert could only whimper as blow by blow Edward delivered hard kicks making Albert eventually pass out. The noise must have startled Elizabeth who came running down the path and she could see for herself Albert lying on the floor.

'Albert,' she called out then ran towards him.

Edward could see she still had the gun and wondered if she had accomplished what she had started and that now Mary was lying on the floor like Albert only dead. He put this thought out of his head as he needed his wits about him and right now, he had to deal with a cunning killer who also had the advantage of having a loaded pistol.

Edward felt in his jacket pocket and could still feel the letter opener that he'd manage to take from the main house.

It felt ridiculously small in comparison to the pistol that Elizabeth had but the blade was sharp, he knew that if he could just aim for Elizabeth's neck or chest that he was in with a chance.

Elizabeth turned and was looking away from Edward and this was the very opportunity he needed. In one fail swoop Edward took the makeshift knife and plunged it into Elizabeth's neck. Nothing happened at first and to Edward's horror Elizabeth's index finger started to tighten on the pistol but blood had now started to ooze out of the wound in her neck and her finger trembled as a result. Both hands now shook violently and she eventually released the gun which dropped clattering onto the floor. It was more luck on Edward's part that the wound from the knife had struck a vital part of the vessels around the neck and was slowly cutting off all life to the body.

Elizabeth was dying a slow death and although she was fighting for her life, it was a futile battle. She had lived in pain twisted by bitterness and now she was about to die a terrible tortured death as it looked like she would die with the same cruelty she had inflicted so horrendously on others.

Edward felt that at last justice was served and he felt nothing but contempt for her as she drew her last breath. Edward could only think that her death was too kind and quick for the pure evilness of her heinous crimes.

As the last part of life was heard disappearing from Elizabeth's body, Edward heard footsteps coming from behind him, they were too loud to belong to Mary and Edward knew instantly that they were a man's and belonged to Albert. Within seconds he'd thrown himself on top of Elizabeth's body and somehow retrieved the pistol and as he turned Albert pushed Edward hard to the ground. The two men fought each other in what was becoming a terrible battle both not willing to give way. Then to Edward's horror Albert somehow managed to get the letter opener from Elizabeth's body in his hand and was aiming it centimetres away from his right eye.

In desperation Edward managed to put out his arm to stop Albert and the two men's strength counterbalanced so that the blade did not move for a few seconds which seemed to Edward as minutes. Suddenly he managed with one massive pull of strength to push Albert's arm out of the way. Albert though was stronger and quicker than he looked and now somehow within seconds, he had his hands around Edward's neck and his grip was tightening fast.

Edward felt like he was choking and the more he struggled the tighter the grip became almost like a tight noose around his neck. Edward started to feel light headed and thought he was about to pass out but sheer force and determination stopped him. Just as the might in his body had almost given up and he had resigned himself to die, he heard a shot and could see blood splattering on the far side of the wall. At first, he thought it was his own blood but soon realised much to his great relief that it was Albert's.

Albert had been shot clean through the chest. Edward pushed his body away from Albert and rolled over, his body stiff and cumbersome. He looked up and saw Mary standing in front of him rigid with the pistol in her hand, she was shaking violently with tears streaming down her face. Edward slowly wracked by pain managed to get up and stepped towards Mary, gently taking the gun away from her gripped hands and took her in his arms.

While she sobbed, he turned around to make sure that Albert was dead. Thankfully his body was motionless and Edward knew at least for a while they were safe. Albert's body had fallen just a foot away from Elizabeth's and both bodies lay side by side.

Ironically, they'd wanted to be together more for money than love and through their acts of cruel callousness they were now united but only in death. Edward shuddered to think what had happened and more importantly what could have happened. He hugged Mary but knew the victory was short lived as they still had to negotiate their way out of the Hall's grounds without both Bella and Howarth seeing them.

'Do you think you can walk?' Edward asked kindly steadying Mary and putting his jacket around her to help take away some of the shock as she was still shaking violently.

'Yes, I'm as good as can be, I just want to be safe, please help me to feel safe.' Mary looked to be in shock. 'Where is Jimmy?'

'He's been hurt but he'll live.'

'Are you sure? We must go to him. '

'No, we must go to safety.'

Mary gripped Edward's hand and Edward worried that Mary might not be strong enough to escape with him. He had to get her out of here and his mind started to think of ideas of trying to escape.

'We can do this together,' Edward said kindly as he formulated a plan that he hoped somehow he could pull off.

'Edward, thank you for saving me,' Mary whispered. 'I wouldn't be alive if it wasn't for you, my father would be so proud of you, you're a real hero.'

'We're not by any means out of the woods yet,' Edward pointed out feeling at that moment not one bit a hero and thinking desperately what to do next for the best.

'At least we've made it this far,' Mary pointed out whilst still holding Edward's hand tightly.

'Can we not go to the Hall for help?'

'I'm sorry Mary but Howarth and his men are there and besides I'm not sure who we can trust.'

'I can't believe Albert did this and the woman, who was she? How can they behave so terribly and I'd no idea Albert was capable of doing such dreadful things, I simply can't believe I ever married him?'

Naturally Mary wanted to ask questions but right now Edward's mind was only on one thing and that was getting out of there alive.

'I'll explain what I know as we go along,' Edward promised hoping that Mary was up to what lay ahead.

# Chapter 20

Edward's throat was hurting more than he liked to admit from the grip of Albert's hands and his head throbbed so much that he hoped he wouldn't pass out, not to mention the fact that he was covered from head to toe with blood stains but he knew no matter what had happened, they now had to get out of the grounds and that meant getting to the outer perimeter of the estate.

Although the entire estate was protected by a high stone wall, on the east side there was if he recalled correctly a small country road that eventually led to the main road to Whitby, which Edward reckoned was about a six mile run give or take.

It was a lot to ask of Mary to walk to the other side of the estate as they would have to cover ground quickly in case Howarth and Bella came looking for them. He thought about this and realised that when Albert and Elizabeth didn't come back, Howarth would soon send a search party to the Lodge and find the two dead bodies. It would be a good idea to put the bodies in the shrubbery hiding them from Howarth. Edward was now in a dilemma as doing this would slow them down by hiding the bodies but it might buy them time later whilst Howarth looked for Elizabeth and Albert.

'Mary do you think you can help me move the bodies, at least then when Howarth comes he might not put two and two together for a while?'

'I can't stand this, Edward, it's just too much,' Mary sobbed and looked truly dreadful by all what had happened.

'We've got to stay strong Mary,' Edward could see that he was going to have to help Mary through this step by step if they were to get to the main road.

Mary started to sob. 'I'm so sorry Edward, I feel somehow that I must be to blame.'

Edward took Mary's arm. 'None of this is your fault, you must remember that you can't let them destroy you because if they catch you, I can guarantee that they'll not think twice and they will kill you, do you understand what I'm telling you Mary?'

Mary nodded and stopped crying. 'I'll try,' she said taking a deep breath.

Edward couldn't help but feel nothing but pity for Mary. She didn't even now know half the treachery and lies that he'd uncovered and he feared that when she did know the truth, it might just do the job that her mother and cruel step sister had set out to do, that is kill her. He knew he'd have to be strong for her and already in his mind he was thinking of taking her to live with Verity, himself and the twins in Sussex and getting as far away from the Hall as possible, that's if they ever made it from here. He also hoped that Jimmy would be alright. Mary would need him after this.

'We'll do the best we can, right now we need to focus,' Edward said bending down and reaching Albert's arms.

Dead bodies are always a weight but as far as Edward was concerned Albert's body seemed to be the weight of at least two men. He somehow along with Mary managed to drag the body over to the bushes and roll it into the dense shrubbery. Thankfully Elizabeth's body was much lighter and they found an equally good hiding place. They managed to clear the blood stains the best they could with a wet cloth. The pistol and letter opener they hid in another part of the hedgerow just by the side of the kitchen window.

They worked silently together, neither of them wanting to speak as they set about trying to clear the gruesome crime scene. If truth be known it was too terrible a task to be able to find the right words to say so both thought it best to remain silent whilst harbouring their own private nightmares.

Within ten minutes the area looked presentable as though nothing untoward had ever happened. They quickly grabbed a small amount of food and some water in a bottle which Mary put in a small wicker basket. Edward slipped his shoes back on and they took a small blanket just in case they needed to rest or to spend the night out in the open.

Edward's plan now was to head towards a small cottage which was in the opposite direction of Herron Village. Stan and Ida had lived there before Mary was born paying rent to David. David had always kept the rent low and in return they gave produce to the Green estate. David's kindness was about to be put to the test as Edward knew that in some ways it was their only hope to get to Whitby.

Mary had told David that Stan owned a car that never ventured out as he'd lost the use of his right hand from fighting at the front but as far as Mary knew the car even after all these years was still road worthy. If they could persuade him to borrow the car then that might take them into Whitby, from there if Edward was lucky, he might be able to contact inspector Dudley. To stay at the Hall was too dangerous.

Edward decided using the phone line was too risky as the Lodge line fed into the main line of the house, which meant that phone calls could be intercepted giving Howarth the advantage of eavesdropping on any conversation.

There was a slight chance that Inspector Dudley was part of this crime but Edward doubted it from his previous dealings with him. Edward was usually a good judge of character and felt that Dudley was not in cahoots with Howarth. Edward had noted that Dudley had acted nonchalant to his London superior. Edward suspected that Dudley had been a good local bobby who over time had risen the up the ranks of the law to then be promoted to only find himself sitting bored behind a desk.

It was a chance Edward knew he'd have to take but to stay here or trust any other police officer associated with Howarth seemed far more dangerous. It was a matter of two evils and right now any plan that involved getting out of there seemed a very good idea.

The weather had been unpredictable all day and again the clouds looked angry and grey as Edward and Mary made their way through the fields which luckily were fairly easy to wade through despite all the rain that had fallen over the last few weeks.

As they went along the fields there were several stiles to climb and Edward had to help Mary who seemed more and more unsteady and weak on her feet. After what seemed to have taken forever they eventually reached a field where Edward had consciously marked as half way.

Edward knew they were short on time but felt it necessary to stop allowing them to take a small break to drink and rest. Mary wanted to sit longer and Edward had to persuade her to get up as he knew they had to keep moving, every minute was vital to get to the farm.

The sea wind was blowing quite strong and Mary put the blanket over her shoulders to stop herself shivering. Exhausted and hungry, at last they reached the brow of the hill where they could see the tiny holding below them. Edward took a good look helped by his vantage point before venturing down. He wanted to know exactly what to do once he got there. It looked like there were some lock up garages to the side of the cottage which Edward presumed held the tractors and hopefully the car that Mary had mentioned.

By this time as they went down the hill, they half walked and half ran at the same time but Edward suddenly pushed Mary into the long grass and dived next to her. A car was now just turning into the forecourt of the farm and Edward could just make out the man getting out of the car followed by two police officers, it was just as he had predicted, Howarth.

'It's Howarth, they've obviously worked out what went on at the Lodge, heaven knows how they've tracked us here, Howarth's a cunning old fox but that doesn't help us right now,' Edward said as much to himself as Mary, whilst getting up.

He felt quite desperate now by the situation they found themselves in. As Edward was considering his next move, he was somewhat surprised by Mary's idea. He thought she'd just about given up hope but as Edward knew there was something about the human spirit that when you have nothing to lose that's when you try the most.

'If we go around the back of the cottage, the farm is on a hill. The garage doors open either side from what I can remember. As a young girl I used to play with their daughter Edith West. I knew the farm well.

We can run the car down the hill some way without actually starting the engine, well enough for it to get us onto the main road to Whitby without anyone knowing, that's if we can manage not to be spotted in the meantime.'

'Mary well done,' Edward said and smiled for the first time in a while. 'I think your plan may just work. If not, we've nothing to lose.'

'We've got to chance it,' Mary said also smiling and looking slightly better.

Edward was impressed by Mary's plan. It was risky but at least once they were in the car, they stood more of a chance than out here in the open, caught in the fields without any back up.

'Ok, but we'll have to be careful not to be spotted, does Stan ever lock the doors to the garage?'

'No,' Mary answered. 'There's no need, it's not really visited by anyone, Edward this isn't London.'

'Yes,' Edward said. 'Er ...but you seem to have your share of crime nonetheless.'

It was a tactless comment but the serialism of the sequence of past events had left Edward's nerves in tatters and the humour felt almost a relief, he looked at Mary not sure of her reaction but he need not have feared as it was just the tonic she needed and she simply smiled back and for that moment at least he felt that they had a fighting chance.

Slowly they both crept down the hill and just as Mary had promised the garage had two entrances. Edward nervously peered over the grass being careful not to be caught, he slowly crawled making sure he made no sudden movements.

'I'm praying the car will be there,' he said nervously as he knew this was perhaps their only chance of a quick getaway.

'I'm certain it will be there, I cannot see any reason why not,' Mary said confidently but at the same time secretly crossed both her fingers.

At first glance Edward couldn't see any sign of the car and a thought suddenly struck him that there was always the possibility that the vehicle would be blocked by the farming equipment but as luck would have it, the car was stacked at the back of the garage or for them, it was at their front.

The next problem would be not if the car was locked but if the keys had not been left in the ignition. Edward knew that if this was the case, he could always hot rod the engine, a trick he'd learnt from a friend back home whose father owned a garage. He could do this when they needed the engine to run later. After a few nervous tense moments, Mary and Edward managed to make it into the garage undetected and just as Edward had anticipated the car key had been left in the ignition.

Edward didn't need to start the car because the incline of the hill was enough for the car to drop gently downwards but the incline was not too steep to cause the steering wheel to start to lose control. Mary carefully got in the car and Edward started to push from the back of the vehicle. At first the car's weight seemed overwhelming but after several attempts from Edward who felt by now utterly exhausted, at last the car loosened and the wheels slowly began to move forwards.

Not wasting a moment, Edward immediately jumped in the car and it then started to pick up speed which was forced by the momentum of the hill. It was also fortunate that the hill went away from the house as when they looked back Howarth's car hadn't moved meaning he was still inside probably cross examining Stan and Ida who thankfully knew nothing they could tell. As Edward was only to aware the police have a way of getting the truth out of someone but if that someone doesn't know anything then they can't tell anything.

Although the car was moving very slowly, it soon gathered enough pace to be able to make it safely and more importantly quietly away from the farm, not starting the engine straight away may have saved their lives. Edward looked behind him to see if they'd been spotted but thankfully up to now they'd got away without been seen or heard thanks for the car being quiet. For the moment at least, luck at last appeared to be on their side and right now they needed it in abundance.

As soon as they hit the country road, Mary hit the brakes causing the car to stop. After swapping seats to let Edward drive, Edward turned the key but he suddenly had a terrible feeling and started to panic as there might be no petrol in the car. At first the car didn't start so he pulled the choke right out and revved the engine, after several false attempts eventually he could hear the noise of the car's engine and much to his relief, the petrol gauge shifted slightly, how reliable it was would be was a different matter but for now at least the car was moving and more importantly away from the Hall.

'It's not too far now Mary, you're bearing up wonderfully in the circumstances,' Edward remarked.

The initial shock had started to wear off and Mary's practical determined nature now started to come through making her feel stronger.

'Hopefully I don't think we're being followed and if things go well for us, we should make it to Whitby, let's just hope we have enough petrol,' Edward said as he checked the petrol gauge again hoping that the arrow showed the correct amount.

'Do you think we will make it?' Mary asked as she wrapped the blanket around her.

Edward was driving but still took Mary's hand that was shaking slightly.

'I know we will and that somehow we will be alright,' he answered reassuringly.

Edward reckoned they now had about a ten mile journey ahead of them and as the car jerked round the sharp bends of the lanes, he began to relax. He knew at least they had put some distance between themselves and Howarth.

As Whitby Abbey came into view, Edward felt utterly relieved but in some ways his troubles had only just begun. Edward wondered what to do for the best, walking straight into a police station to admit killing two people didn't seem the most rational thing to do, especially by then making the story totally unbelievable by saying that one of the Chief Senior Officers of the Met was as bent as a crow bar and also was the mastermind for smuggling diamonds into the country and also for killing two people.

After mulling his thoughts over and getting the feeling that they were up against all odds he told Mary to get the few belongings she had out of the car. It seemed to abandon the car was the most logical thing to do and they would then walk the rest of the way into the small seaside town.

After parking the car on a narrow side street far away from the main road into the little town, Mary and Edward passed the sea front. Although the mood between them was tense, Edward allowed himself a quick glance at the sea as it served never to disappoint, the North Sea always has a beauty of its own. Renowned for its rocky inlets and rugged coastline it has a certain magical appeal and none so much as today.

Edward couldn't help feel slightly envious as he spotted a family with three small children playing innocently in the sand. He felt it should be him with Verity and the twins but right now he wasn't even sure if he'd ever see them again. He tried to put all thoughts to one side as he needed to be strong and think clearly.

He grabbed Mary's hand impulsively, he'd now been given the impetus he needed to get to Whitby Police Station and with a renewed vigour and strength he started to run with Mary, supporting her by linking arms trying to help her as much as he could.

'You're doing so well Mary, I'm very proud of you,' Edward said as he squeezed Mary's hand. Although she didn't answer, she managed to squeeze it back and at that point this made Edward feel an enormous sense of responsibility.

It was then that he heard the distinct sound of a car's engine and when he looked back, he saw a black car behind them. He expected it to be Howarth but was relieved to see it wasn't. Feeling slightly more confident, he then turned around again only to now see that the car was already beginning to slow down as it neared them.

'Mary, don't look now but there's a car that's just pulled up, I'm sorry but I think it's them, we've got to quicken our pace,' Edward spoke quickly worrying that they wouldn't be able to outrun the car and he quickened his pace. He started to look for side streets or alleyways that they could duck into.

'Quick let's take a shortcut,' Edward beckoned for Mary to follow.

They both ran into a narrow cobbled street just to the side of them, which looked like it led towards the harbour. Edward took a gamble as he thought that the car would not follow them down the little street as the car was too wide. Edward was looking frantically to find the police station which Mary had said was just behind the Abbey itself.

'I think for the moment at least, we're safe for now,' Edward said trying to get his breath back.

'I doubt it Edward, Whitby is only a small place, if they know the roads and layout then I'm afraid they'll soon find us,' Mary pointed out equally panting from running so quickly.

'How far do you reckon to the police station?' Edward asked beginning to feel exhausted by the day's events.

'A few minutes walk if that.'

'Let's hope we can get there before the car does,' Edward said realising that although they were only minutes from some degree of safety, danger seemed much closer.

When they started to walk down the street, they soon saw as they turned the corner, that the same black car was now suspiciously parked blocking their path. It was too late to run, Edward knew it was a futile task to go anywhere as the car would just speed up and it was impossible to outrun it. The game was up and there was nothing he or Mary could do about it. They would just have to accept whatever Howarth would punish them with.

Edward's mind started to visualise being slowly tortured by Howarth who was obviously a cruel man that was both devious and plainly quite evil. He just hoped for Mary's sake whatever he had in store for them it would be quick.

He had just taken one step forwards towards the car and heard a voice that he didn't expect to hear, it was not the voice of Howarth but Dudley instead. As first Edward thought he must be somehow involved with Howarth and grabbed Mary to protect her.

'It's alright,' Dudley shouted. 'You're both safe now, I know all about Howarth and everything that has happened to you both. We know you're both innocent and you both have nothing to fear but we do need to get you off the streets and quickly before Howarth finds you.'

'How can we trust you?' Edward asked unsure of what to think about Dudley's motives.

'You have to trust us, you have no choice, you'll have to come with us or both your lives are in danger and I cannot then protect you.'

Edward wanted to believe Dudley but after everything that had happened, injured and in shock, his instincts now were of suspicion. After all it was quite feasible that Dudley and Howarth were in this together, both of them literally knee deep, in fact at the moment Edward thought waist high was a better description of the situation.

Dudley could see Edward hesitating and tried a different tack. 'You have a straight choice you either come with us or Howarth will inevitably pick you up.'

'How did you find us?' Edward said suspiciously.

It was Jimmy, he regained consciousness and found his father George. They managed to sneak out of the Hall into the village to make the telephone call. It was risky as they could have been followed.'

Mary's face softened when she heard Jimmy's name. 'Is he alright, is he injured?' Mary asked hoping that nothing terrible had happened to him.

'It seems young Jimmy is a very lucky man. He has as many lives as cat, all of which is fortunate for a police officer.' Dudley allowed himself to smile and then added. 'I do think that after this he will be needing someone to look after him. He's a tough man but all tough men need some comfort.'

Dudley looked at Mary who nodded.

Throughout her short marriage to Albert, Mary had never once stopped thinking about Jimmy. She could never tell anybody but she wished she'd had an opportunity to marry him instead of Albert. To her it had always been Jimmy. Opportunities do not come in abundance in life and Mary was not going to waste one more precious second. If Jimmy wanted her then she was his, that she was sure of.

Time ticked on and Dudley had to act quickly. Edward and Mary still stood unable to think and Dudley recognised that they were both in deep shock. He signalled for two officers from the car to get out and help them to the police vehicle.

'I know you've been through a lot but right but now I need you both to be safe,' Dudley explained and paused allowing them to understand what he was telling them and then went on. 'There's a lot of information I need to get from you both and to pass on to you but for now that can wait.'

Mary and Edward had both resigned themselves to the dreadful fact that they had nowhere to run and seemed to accept their fates. Mary like Edward was also very wary of Dudley. Howarth had not only let them down but had turned out to be part of theses terrible crimes and both felt that Dudley could also be implicated.

'How do we know you'll not hurt us?' Edward asked.

'You don't and can't possibly know for sure so you'll just have to trust your instincts.'

Edward turned to Mary. 'We don't have to get in, it's your call.'

'I think we should,' Mary answered relieved that some form of closure was coming even if that happened to be a bad thing.

'Ok, if that's alright with you, then we'll go to the police station with you,' said Edward already helping Mary to the car. 'Mary will need some medical attention, she's very weak from what has happened.'

Edward looked at Dudley hoping that he was as good as his word. Right now, he needed Mary to eat and keep her strength up. They both sat in the back of the car and after a few minutes Edward admitted to himself that he now felt safer than before. Dudley sat at the front of the car in the passenger side and was quiet at the start of the journey but slowly started to chat although preferring to only make pleasantries. Edward listened as he started to drift off to sleep, he was therefore surprised and somewhat startled when Dudley announced their whereabouts.

'We are not going to Whitby Police Station but the one at Thirsk. There you will be assigned with an officer who will give you fresh clothes and you will both be given the chance to clean yourselves and eat before we have a very informal chat.'

As he said this both Mary and Edward looked down at their clothes and realised for the first time that were both soaked in blood as well as mud and tears.

'Once you've had something to eat and drink then I'll tell you as much information about this case as we know but for now, we've got an hour's drive so if you can just try and relax as much as I hope you can.'

'Thank you,' Mary said as she closed her eyes and realised just how tired she was, within a few minutes she was fast asleep.

It was difficult to still not feel anxious but as the car journey went on, Edward felt at last that they would be safe. He didn't take much notice of the lovely countryside that passed them or the glimpses every now of the coast line. After what seemed an endlessly long journey with Mary half asleep and occasionally breaking down in tears, they at last arrived in Thirsk.

True to his word Mary and Edward were given food and a chance to change clothes and slowly started to feel something like their old selves again.

There was something clinical yet primitive about getting rid of the blood stained clothes and both Mary's and Edward's mood lifted immediately. Instead of being taken into one of the formal interview rooms, they were taken into Dudley's office where a fresh pot of tea welcomed them. Dudley politely chatted to Mary and nodded to Edward.

'Before I begin, I just want to say how terribly sorry I am for all that you've both had to endure. I can only offer my sincere condolences and the fact that you are both safe now but you've both been through a terrible ordeal and one that you're not likely to forget for the rest of your lives.'

Edward looked at Mary and thought that what Dudley had just said would be true. He knew himself that somehow this would change his life forever and Mary's life had now changed so dramatically that even if she wanted her life as she knew it, that life had now gone.

'It seems that a terrible crime has been committed over the course of what you both think is a few months but in fact this terrible sinister plot has been planned and the seeds sown for many years now and I feel you both need an explanation to try to come to terms with what has happened,' Dudley said sympathetically.

'I don't quite understand when you say this has been going on for years, how can that be?' Mary said thoughtfully thinking that perhaps her life as she'd known it so far had been totally false.

'This is a tale which I'm sure you both can fill in the gaps as we go along but by in large it started twenty five years ago and primarily involves your mother Mary, who was then known as Lady Isabella Crawley.'

As Dudley spoke he took the liberty of pouring them both some tea and put two sugar cubes in his own cup. Dudley shuffled his notes on his desk as if thinking where exactly to start the story.

'Your mother was incredibly beautiful and wealthy as I'm sure you're aware of and at that time was indeed a real catch in society especially with her aristocratic connections, this made her even more attractive especially as a suitable wife. Her life was perfect in every way and to add icing on the cake, she was all set to marry the Duke of Northumberland but as the wedding came closer, she got cold feet and nagging doubts about the union. She felt not ready to settle down and longed for excitement and adventure.

Having a change of mind, didn't bode well to the young Duke at all as you can imagine and so it was that by the shame of your mother's actions, your grandparents thought it best that she should be sent away to a finishing school in Switzerland to let the dust settle so to speak.

At the time it seemed a good move and by all accounts your mother loved it there but her head was soon turned by a rather dashing young man called Ethan Wood. He was a cad at the best but had a liking for the finer things in life, women, drink and a deadly habit to gamble.

Your mother wouldn't have been the first or last woman to be duped by his charms and soon realised that she had been foolish at best and soon saw him for what he was but it would seem that circumstances took an unusual twist and by then it was too late to be totally rid of him as she found herself let's say in the family way.'

'I have a brother or sister?' Mary managed to say.

'I'll come to that in a minute, but yes, your grandparents were furious with the news as was to be expected. We have to see things from their point of view, firstly she'd turned down the most eligible bachelor it would seem of the day and then she'd been an incredibly stupid young woman and found herself in an appalling embarrassing situation not suited for a young lady from such a prestigious background.

Your grandfather of course immediately told her that the baby must go but your grandmother was catholic and wouldn't allow an abortion, so your mother was sent away from Switzerland. After a great deal of thought, it was decided that she would extend her stay abroad and live with some relatives just by Lake Como. Here she could be hidden away from the rest of the world and nobody in their social circles would need to know.

After nine months Isabella came home and the baby girl was named Elizabeth. Elizabeth would stay with the family in Italy and be raised as their own child,' Dudley paused to take a breath.

'Elizabeth was the girl with the auburn hair that was at the Hall with Albert, the one that was killed wasn't she... er... but I still don't see how this all fits together?' Mary asked more puzzled than ever and desperately trying to make sense of it all.

'Yes, that's correct and your mother in fairness part played along with her parents and after the birth came dutifully back to England, where it seems your parents had already lined a up suitable partner for her and of course this time she did not dare to refuse and the man's name was David, your father.

For the first few years of marriage the truth of the past remained only between your grandparents, mother and the family in Italy and as the saying goes, no one would have been any the wiser but the thing with secrets is that there was always somebody they'd forgotten about and somehow Ethan, we are not sure why, found out about his daughter Elizabeth and more importantly just how wealthy your grandparents were. Ethan was heavily in debt as always and I'm afraid the temptation for blackmail was too irresistible and it seems that before long, your grandparents were sending large amounts of money over to the Italian Lakes, which I'm afraid in time became more and more frequent which helped to pay his heavy gambling debts.'

'But I never knew anything about this, nobody has ever told me any of this story,' Mary said wondering if her father had known as well.

'And you would never have known anything of the story as this agreement went on for years and of course in the meantime you were born. As time went by Ethan naturally became greedier than your grandparents ever thought and the vast amounts of money he wanted started to become absurd. It seems in the end they had no choice and refused to pay any longer. They feared of course the worst that everybody in their social circles would find out the truth but just as they braced themselves for this, ironically Ethan found out that he had terminal cancer of the brain. As if by some miracle he became a changed man overnight and went on surprisingly to live another year, never asking for another payment from your grandparents but his dying wish was to make sure that Elizabeth knew exactly who her rightful parents were not just her mother but her father as well.

Out of the blue, one day in late autumn when Elizabeth was just ten years old Ethan turned up in England with Elizabeth demanding a place in your mother's life. We don't really have the exact facts of what took place but it seems that Elizabeth there and then became a part of Bella's life on the basis she was hidden away and was sent to boarding school. As far as we know David knew nothing about Elizabeth but in fairness why should he.

Just before Ethan's death, it so happened that he was attacked during a card game that took place in a dingy backstreet bedsit just off the south coast near Portsmouth. The police got involved and your mother was pulled in for questioning not that they thought she was guilty of any crime but just to get an overview of the case. That's when I'm afraid, she met the dashing Detective Howarth. In fairness to your mother, we have to remember, she'd had an arranged marriage to your father and Howarth seemed to represent a life she felt she'd lost or never really had.

What she couldn't have known is that no matter how bad Ethan was, Howarth was far worse. He was already as bent as they come and he saw in Bella, a path into the top layers of society. Howarth over the years had started his life as a police officer and soon mingled this with a life of crime forming a small protection racket that he'd helped form in the East End. He went on to bigger exploits, selling drugs and as we know his last venture for the past ten years or more was diamond smuggling, said to be worth thousands of pounds even at today's prices.

This information about Howarth is highly embarrassing to the police force as you can imagine, we discovered his other life a few years ago and exactly what that entailed. We used him to get as much information as we needed. Only a few very senior officers knew of this, not many including Jimmy. It was very unfortunate what happened to him.

It seems that after the dalliance with Ethan and then having to marry David, your mother was left feeling confused and feeling betrayed and she consequently threw herself into Howarth's life in every way. I'm afraid we've found out that she even eventually became a courier herself and was often used to meet clients in exclusive clubs in London.'

'Yes, now that I come to think of it, I remember my mother went to London quite a lot, she said it was for her charity work and she would spend sometimes a few days or even a few weeks in the city. I always worried about her and what she was doing but I would have never of guessed this not in a million years,' Mary said acknowledging by shaking her head.

'Elizabeth by now had become a young woman and became a big part of Bella's life and she lived with Howarth sometimes in the week along with Elizabeth and even partly in the holidays almost as a family. As Elizabeth grew up so did her ambitions and she desperately wanted to compete with you Mary in every way. A husband who was rich and successful became almost an obsession and your mother promised to find someone that she could marry who was very wealthy.

History however has a canny way to repeat itself and she should have been wary by her own poor lack of judgement in the past as this caused her to find the worst of husbands for Elizabeth. The Smithers' family resembled both Ethan and Howarth rolled into one. Elizabeth quickly found that she was married to someone who was totally false and in reality, hadn't got a penny to their name,' Dudley said as he paused his story and there was a silence in the room as people digested the tale.

'I can't believe that my mother virtually led a double life,' Mary said trying to take in all the details of the story.

'It is a truly terrible tale,' Dudley said sympathetically. 'Would you like me to carry on, we can take a rest if you need one, it's understandable?'

'No, I think I need to know all the story, it's important to me, I've got to face the truth sooner or later no matter how difficult it is to hear,' Mary noted more to herself than to Dudley.

'Elizabeth was desperate to succeed in life and realising that she was looking at a life of poverty, Albert quickly became part of Howarth's diamond smuggling ring. It was a foolish move, as we were aware of some of Howarth's activities by then and therefore made it virtually impossible for them to gain any money from their dealings. As we'd now become aware of their criminal activities, we used them only to give us names in the bargain and kept quiet hoping that we could arrest the criminals higher up the food chain so to speak.'

Edward interrupted. 'Did you ever suspect David or myself?'

'Yes, we have to suspect everyone and then rule them out. We never really thought David or yourself were involved but we couldn't rule it out. You have our sincere apologies but we needed to keep an interest in all people connected to Smithers so Mary even your father was investigated but he was far too smart to be involved. I'm so sorry for what happened to him, it was a cruel twist of fate.'

Edward nodded. 'You couldn't be there all the time, it was inevitable someone was going to get hurt,' Edward spoke softly.

'It was at this point that Elizabeth devised a cunning cruel plan to take everything from you. Firstly, she would kill your father as this would allow you Mary to inherit everything and by this time if you were married to Albert, then if anything happened to you, then it meant that Albert got the lot and then could remarry Elizabeth and all your money would be hers.'

Mary pulled her cardigan around herself tightly and Edward reached over to hold her hand. He wanted Mary to take a break even for a few minutes but she was determined to hear the story through. Edward acknowledged to himself just how brave she was by listening to the gruesome tale, he only hoped she could remain so afterwards.

'But surely if Albert was married to Elizabeth then he couldn't marry me which would have made the marriage illegal and then all this plan would have been in vain?' Mary pointed out.

'No, that's the thing, Elizabeth and Albert have been divorced for over a year now. This was a plan remember that they'd made over a few years and one that was put together methodically. It was a plan that had all the makings of a proper criminal's mind and both Howarth and Albert I'm afraid, fit that bill perfectly.'

'But Betty, I don't understand, why did she have to die? ' Mary asked.

'I'm afraid to say that it was the case of wrong place wrong time, she was the classic story of a victim of crime just as your father was.'

Edward sat and listened intently, he'd been lucky enough to at least know some of the case before he'd got to the station unlike poor Mary where all this information was new to her. Edward however was puzzled by just how much Dudley knew about Bella's story.

'Forgive me but how do you know all this story in so much detail?' Edward asked curiously without doubting Dudley's honesty.

There was a silence in the room and Dudley spoke gently not wanting to upset Mary anymore.

'We got Howarth, we picked him up at the farm, in fact that's when we saw you take the car from the lock up garage but we had other things on our mind and guessed correctly that you'd be heading to Whitby,' Dudley said and put his hands through his hair which was a habit Edward thought he must do when he was deep in thought.

'We also picked up your mother, she was understandably very upset and wanted to know if you were alive, if it's any consolation she desperately wanted me to tell you that she's been an absolute fool. She told me she loves you and wished more than anything she could put things right. She wanted to make this confession to tell you how this sorry story came about.'

Dudley got up from his seat and walked towards the window. Edward knew he was stalling for time not wanting to say something. Edward half guessed what was about to come but when Dudley said it, it was still a shock.

'It was just as we we're about to put her in the car,' Dudley paused again and his hand shot through his hair. 'Your mother... she pulled a gun from her handbag, at first we thought she was going to take a shot at us to try and escape but she pulled the gun to herself and the bullet went through her own head.'

'My mother killed herself?' Mary said in disbelief thinking that she'd lost both parents in the most tragic of circumstances in less than a few weeks.

As Mary sat there in Dudley's office, she thought back to the part of the story where her mother had been sent to Lake Como and it was obvious to her that the young Isabella that was sent as a young girl to Italy, was then sadly turned and tainted by men who abused her.

'Yes, if it's any consolation, as I've said, none of what I say can change any of this but I think she loved you but like all criminals, life had made her what she'd become. She'd chosen wrongly in her life and was easily swayed by other people especially falling for men who would only hurt her. Her downfall in life was having too much and other people taking it away from her and abusing her along the way.'

Edward put his hands in his head, he'd always loved his brother, there was an eight year difference between them but right now it might as well have been a hundred. He no longer had his brother and a trail of devastation was left behind. He didn't know how to start to put things right but he had to for Mary's sake. He wondered what had caused Bella's terrible behaviour perhaps it was as Dudley had said that she was too weak and gave into temptation too readily.

He thought of his own beautiful wife who was so unselfish and he knew always put his children first before anything and then his thoughts turned to poor Mary who'd been brought up in a household full of deceit. David, he suspected deep down must have known some of the story but out of decency for his daughter had probably decided to turn a blind eye.

Edward couldn't help feel how fragile people were, life was very complex, it made some people have good values and ideas and others give way into giddy thoughts and fantasies showing weakness. He shuddered and realised that he now had to put matters right. By now Dudley had gone to get another drink and he was left alone with Mary in the room.

'Mary, they'll be lots of legal matters that we'll need to deal with but you know I'm here to help but no matter what happens, I insist that you are to come back home with me to Sussex and stay at least for the time being with Verity and the kids.'

'I can't leave all this, my father would have wanted me here to take care of things at the Hall, there's the business to manage,' Mary pointed out.

Edward spoke softly. 'No that's where you're wrong Mary, he would have wanted you right away from here, far away from the bad memories and to be completely safe so that no one can ever hurt you again.'

Mary smiled and nodded.

'Before I go, I need to see Jimmy.' Mary's face blushed but now she'd said her feelings out loud so she went on. 'If there's any future for us, then I have to give it a go. You understand don't you. Edward some damned good has to come from this otherwise…' she paused. 'Otherwise there's just no point.'

Mary started to cry which was unsurprising in the circumstances.

'I understand more than you'll ever know Mary. Take your time but we're here for you.'

Edward took Mary's hand and squeezed it. A little hope passed between them and for now it was a great comfort.

Dudley had now sat back at the table and Edward felt he ought to ask the question that had been nagging him throughout the story.

'Is the estate Mary's or because of Bella's behaviour and involvement in the diamonds will the estate be taken away from her?' Edward wanted to know where Mary stood in terms of money.

Dudley shuffled his papers once more. 'The only good news is that your father never had any connection with the smuggling of any diamonds. His businesses will remain intact and without question of any wrong doings. Your father actually was a kind man and it seemed donated a considerable amount of money to various charities. He was by all accounts, some say a lot like your grandfather, something of a philanthropist.'

Mary smiled, so he had been a lot like her grandfather and how she wished her mother had been so.

'As far as I'm concerned you are both now free to leave when you wish. You are welcome to stay here at the station as long as you feel necessary and then I will arrange for you to be taken wherever you want and there's no reason to fear any reprimands, you're both safe and free to go.'

A few hours passed until Mary and Edward came out of the station and took it upon themselves to simply stand by the sea wall with the sea breeze blowing on their faces. It felt refreshing to have the sea around them. Both of them knew in that instant that their lives could never be the same after everything that had happened to them. They had both seen and heard too much, especially Mary, for any of the past to seem normal.

As they stood there by the sea, they both agreed there and then that as painful as it might be they had to both go forwards and make some good come of this awful tragedy.

They shook hands on that promise with the Abbey in the background and made a pact that unless they needed to, they would try to never mention to anyone exactly what had happened. They knew it would be difficult but if they were going to have any decent sort of life, it had no place for the evilness and wickedness that had descended on Herron Hall.

It was a few months later as autumn came again and the coast once more took on its remoteness of fog, an eerie breeze swept around the caves and inlets of Whitby. The coastline stood in its timeless natural wild beauty oblivious to the troubled few years of some of its inhabitants. Edward and Mary had made their way northwards and returned to Herron Hall. Both had visited the village but had not set foot in the Hall. It was a visit that both were dreading but both knew was long overdue.

Mary arrived no longer a widow but had since remarried. The wedding had been a private ceremony in the local village church. At the time, it had caused a few mummers but the villagers who knew some of the story where very understanding. It had been attended by only a few with Inspector Dudley of all people being one.

Edward had shed a few tears when Jimmy and Mary had been pronounced man and wife, he had rarely ever cried in his life but emotion had overtaken him. He knew really that he had cried for his brother David and though he was no longer with them, in the church he could have sworn he'd felt his presence that day which had given him some comfort.

Mary still looked gaunt and tired but some of the old Mary shone out, all of which Edward knew was the result of Jimmy's love and devotion for her.

Some of Herron Hall's staff were still employed for the day to day running's of the house but that didn't stop Edward and Mary feeling nervous and not sure of what to expect on their return. As they climbed the steps to the entrance, Edward stopped and looked carefully at his niece who he only had respect and admiration for.

'It's a massive step to come back here Mary, I think you've done the right thing by putting the house on the market to sell,' Edward said reassuringly taking Mary's hand.

'I will still always love it around here and will come to visit but not to the Hall, this is my final goodbye.'

'It has taken everything from you and now it owes you so much. I hope the couple from London will soon put forward a good offer,' Edward said and crossed his fingers as he spoke and hoped it would be soon.

'If they do, it will be fortunate as it's just before winter and you know it's harder to keep running the house during those bleak months,' Mary pointed out practically.

'It's also worked out well that they're willing to take the staff on,' Edward remarked. 'David would be pleased about that, he was always good to his staff.'

They stood at the top of the drive where Edward had stopped the car so they could get a better view of the grand house. Even after all the turmoil, they were both taken aback by just how beautiful the house and grounds looked. The Hall looked undisturbed despite what had happened.

Mary was glad now she had decided to return to the house even if it was for the last time. A part of her was torn as she still loved Herron Hall, she had lived here, grown up there and knew despite everything that had taken place it would always be part of her. She realised she'd of course have to sell it as to live there would be too painful.

Her life had at last been rewarded and she now had a wonderful husband whom she dearly loved. She was six months pregnant and was overjoyed by how life had worked out. She felt truly blessed.

They'd decided to move in entirely new directions going back to her father's family in America on the East coast just near enough to New York. She knew it was just the fresh start they needed. They would still come to visit England and perhaps they would come back up to the North Yorkshire coast and stay with a few good friends in land but she doubted if she or Jimmy would ever return to the Hall itself.

Edward sensed this and decided to give Mary a few hours just to be on her own with Jimmy and to gather any possessions that they wanted to take and more importantly to find some kind of closure if that were possible.

Jimmy walked alongside her which made her feel stronger. His parents no longer worked at the Hall choosing to live nearer Whitby just yards from the beach. He'd left the police force and worked for an uncle of Mary's in Maine where they now lived.

In the end, Mary chose only a few pieces of jewellery that her grandfather had given her from a young girl, making sure that they were light enough to take on her travels, she felt they would make her feel close to her father and grandfather.

Along with Jimmy, they walked around each room to say goodbye even finding time to laugh at childhood memories when they played together. It was a sad moving occasion as goodbyes always are. Each room, every corner or piece of furniture held a memory and became a giant photo album of Mary's past, obviously most of those memories she wanted to erase but that's the thing about the past no matter what we do once something has happened it's becomes part of us good or bad.

The family that had shown interest in the Hall were from London. The firm selling the house felt confident they would offer a good price for all the estate and more importantly to Mary, they seemed nice caring people. Mary could only hope that she could erase the past from the house and take it with her and that it wouldn't haunt the new owners. Of course, no money in the world could ever make up for what Mary had endured but it meant that she was protected from the outside world with enough money to never rely on anyone else.

After a sad couple of hours, they were ready to leave, she met Edward again and they both said goodbyes to a few trusted members of staff and for the very last time they drove down the long tree lined drive. They made a detour to drive past Whitby and Mary couldn't help but admire the historic Abbey dotted on the skyline perhaps a permanent reminder to her of what had happened.

True to the agent's word, within a few months, the family from London moved into the house. At first all was well but the events that had happened couldn't it seem let go and rumours soon surfaced that the house was haunted, many believing that it was the ghost of Bella Green.

She was regularly seen in various rooms throughout the Hall but none so much as surprisingly in David's own walled herb garden outside. To this day it is said that she still haunts the Hall, the staff believing that she is a troubled spirit unable to let go of her terrible past.

# Chapter 21

By this time the train had come to a sudden halt and the noise from the steam outside the carriages seemed deafening. Despite the time of night Hull station seemed very busy made more so by station staff changing shifts as it was just before midnight.

Sophie had listened to Emily throughout all the train journey and apart from the odd question had remained engrossed in the tale. Emily drank her last sips of tea from her cup and placed her cup and saucer neatly at the back of the small makeshift table. Both women took it in turns to get their luggage from the rack above and opened the carriage door. The chill from the night air sent a shiver down Emily's spine.

'It's a cold evening despite the warm day,' Emily said as she reached to put her coat on.

'I think it's because it's a clear night and it's because we're so near to the coast,' Sophie pointed out.

'After you,' Mary said as she let Sophie out of the carriage first.

Sophie dragged her case out of the compartment and suddenly asked. 'It was a remarkable story that you've just told me and thank you for sharing it but by the way I wonder where Mary is now, does she still live over in the states?'

Emily coughed perhaps a reaction to the cold evening. 'Wherever she is, I'm sure as I've said with Jimmy she found a peace that she could live with.'

'Yes, I'm sure she did,' Sophie said more to herself than Emily.

There was a strangeness about Sophie that was made more apparent under the dim station lights. The two women stood aside of the platform and politely shook hands. Emily took her case which was fairly light and walked left towards her accommodation.

Luckily the hotel she'd chosen was just outside the station which was a sensible decision as Hull was a notorious city for sailors and Emily didn't want to risk running into a few drunken men. The Coast Hotel had proven from Emily's last few visits to be a good choice and from what she could remember, the staff were extremely friendly and the hotel beautifully decorated.

It was one of Hull's hidden gems and Emily was grateful to have found such a place when she came back to the North coast. Tomorrow she would catch the small coastal train to stay with her friend. Entering the hotel, it was just as nice as she remembered from a few years ago on her last visit. The reception area seemed to have been refurbished with gold paint which gave the place a more elegant character.

After settling in her room, Emily found that she was rather cold and shut the window. The room soon started to warm up but Emily still couldn't sleep after retelling the story, she felt too unsettled and when daylight broke, she woke early and made her way down to the dining room where she had some light breakfast.

She was hungry after her journey and enjoyed the breakfast helping herself to two pots of freshly brewed tea. She picked the newspaper from the desk and started to read, it was then that she noticed Sophie in the hotel, she was just coming down the stairs. Emily immediately got up to greet her but Sophie seemed preoccupied and even though Emily called her name several times, it was obvious to Emily that she was in a rush to get somewhere.

On the train Sophie had looked different but here just for a few seconds she seemed to recognise her from her own past but couldn't quite place her as to where from.

The little train that went up the coast was virtually empty and although it took a couple of hours, it made for a pleasant journey. It was a lovely sunny warm day and Emily admired the countryside, which was particularly pretty at this time of year, the moors were bathed in heather. The scene almost resembled a painting of a perfect landscape. It wasn't the neat countryside that can be found in the home counties of our country, this was a wild rugged landscape only broken up by ridges on the hills.

At last Emily reached the little village of Helmsley, Susan a friend from her past lived in one of the cottages on the Main Street. The cottage was idyllic and resembled something straight out of a quintessential postcard of British country life. Susan was an elderly lady now but as she came to the door she still looked exactly as she had when she was younger.

The two women spent the day in Susan's garden which was filled with honeysuckle and rose bushes. As it was particularly warm, they ate outside on the lawn and Emily retired early in the small guest room decorated full of flowers and wicker furniture. It was one of those summer evenings when it just wouldn't go dark and even when night time finally came, the brightness of the moon lit up the far side window of her room making shapes on the window panes from the trees outside.

After tossing and turning for the best part of a few hours, Emily felt thirsty and switched on her light to get herself a glass of water from the sink in her room. She stood by the window for a couple of minutes trying to get some fresh air and then went to the sink running the water to try and get it as cold as she could.

Emily had felt very tired as she came to bed and had been keen to get straight to sleep. It was only now as she looked up that she noticed a long mirror placed near the door in her room. For a second she noticed a movement in the mirror which she presumed was from the light of the moon.

She filled her glass with cold water and drank slowly. It was then she heard a noise which seemed to be coming from the corner of the room. She quickly turned and as she did, she glanced at the mirror again and that's when she caught the sight of a figure staring at her from behind. She had to put her hands over her mouth to stop herself from screaming out loud. Her heart raced. As she looked again she could see this time who it was. It seemed unthinkable but it was Sophie.

'Sophie.' Her blood went cold. 'Sophie... er... what are you doing here?' Emily whispered feeling extremely scared and wondering if she could run out of the room quickly.

'I followed you,' came the reply.

'Why?' Emily asked. 'Why would you want to do that?'

'I think you know the answer why. You don't even know who I am do you?'

'Should I?' Emily reasoned.

'Think carefully.'

'I've never seen you before except from our train journey,' Emily answered and then hesitated as Sophie did look familiar in some way.

'Yet I know exactly who you are, Mary.'

Emily winced, she'd not been called that name in a very long time, in fact since she'd gone to America all those years ago and along with her new life with Jimmy she'd changed her name from Mary to Emily. She couldn't believe how Sophie could know that when they had just met from the train journey which they had just shared. Emily tried desperately to think who this woman was and yet there was no apparent connection that she could think of.

'How did you know my real name, I've not been called that in over thirty years since I was a young woman, I've lived in America for twenty-five of those and now live in London with my husband?'

Perhaps it was from living in London that she recognised her, it was after all such a big city that each day it was possible to meet dozens of people and yet never really know them. For a few years she'd worked in a charity organisation for the Salvation Army so maybe it was from there.

'You're Mary Green or was it Mary Smithers?' Sophie demanded.

'Yes, but I still don't understand how you could possibly know that?' Emily protested who had now composed herself enough and had turned to face Sophie who was pointing a small revolver at her.

'Whatever you think, you can't possibly know anything about me,' Emily pointed out feeling her throat tense up.

'Do you not recognise me? '

'No,' Emily said truthfully.

'You killed my mother Elizabeth and my father Albert Smithers,' Sophie said half laughing, she was enjoying this, she'd waited long enough.

'But they had no children?' Emily asked trying quickly to piece everything together.

'Only me, you never thought to ask your mother, while you lived at Herron Hall in all that luxury. I was meanwhile sent to live with a family who were very cruel to me and then lived in orphanages after that.'

'I'm very sorry about that,' Mary spoke softly and was trying now to calm the situation.

'History always repeats itself, your mother abandoned my mother your half-sister, by fate's cruel twist the story just repeated itself. Unlike my mother who was brought up in relative luxury in Italy, I however was sent from one orphanage to another, brutal horrible homes where terrible things happened to me. I would have never known who I was, but one day I happened by chance to see a newspaper cutting about a gruesome set of murders that took place in a beautiful Hall on the North Yorkshire moors.

At the time, the article of course meant nothing to me but on the page, there was a picture of my mother Elizabeth. Call it telepathy or serendipity whatever you want but I couldn't get the picture of the woman in the article out of my mind.'

'It was a cruel way to find out,' Emily sympathised whilst hoping Sophie would put the gun down.

'The photo of the woman literally haunted me. The orphanage where I was at the time was governed by a horrible man but his wife, Matilda was very kind and very educated. Luckily for me I asked about the newspaper article and she promised to find out more about the story in the archives of the local library. Matilda managed to find past newspaper cuttings about the case and with her help we started to piece the story together.

Matilda helped because she pitied me but my efforts became an obsession which filled my every waking hour. It was then that we found out that on my birth certificate my parents were Albert and Elizabeth Smithers, who were the murdered people in the newspaper from Herron Hall.'

'I'd no idea honestly about you, you have to believe me,' was all Emily managed to say.

'When my parents married they managed to keep both their marriage and divorce so much a secret that you never knew about it and Albert my father never told anyone about me as they divorced so quickly. He then set about to take your wealth from you, just as now I'm about to take your life from you.'

'But what good will it do by killing me, what will you achieve?' Emily asked more to herself than Sophie. 'Don't give way to hatred, no good will ever come of it, that I can promise you.'

'You're wrong as it will take away the pain of having no parents and I'll finish the job my mother was unable to do, to kill you.'

As Sophie said this Emily knew it was true, she'd tried over the years to erase the face of Elizabeth from her memory but now seeing Sophie who'd ironically inherited the same auburn hair she realised that Sophie was exactly who she said she was and that right now she was in real danger.

'How did you find me?' Emily was trying to stall for time but for now Sophie was willing to play along with it.

'I read in the articles that the daughter Mary had vanished and nobody knew where but slowly I realised somebody at the Hall or village must know so I worked there and befriended a lovely family who live just outside on the estate itself... and,' Sophie smiled to herself. 'You were foolish to send them Christmas cards and leave your address but even more when you moved back to England.'

'I can't believe you hated me so much,' Emily said.

'I traced you to Kensington and for a good few months have waited for my moment. When I realised that you were planning to travel back to North Yorkshire, you can't imagine the delight when I knew you were seeing a friend not far from Whitby itself. So, I followed you here to Helmsley.'

'There's no need for the gun, please put it away,' Emily said and was desperately trying to reason with Sophie to make her understand.

'No, it finishes tonight, right here, history will restore some justice.'

'What about Susan my friend?' Emily feared the worst. 'Susan worked at the Hall but please don't hurt her, she has no part in any of this,' Emily was pleading now.

'Don't worry my business is not with her but you, you're the one I intend to take down,' Sophie almost hissed.

Emily was desperate by now and couldn't quite believe that she found herself years later having escaped half her life to America to be back near Herron Hall. She was still surrounded by a past she'd tried so hard to escape, this couldn't be happening, not twice.

'Let me go and I'll give you all the money you feel you are owed.'

'I don't need money unlike my mother.' Sophie retorted and flashed a gold band at Emily. 'I married well and I made damned sure that my husband actually had money unlike my father Albert,' Sophie said and laughed.

'There must be something I can give you or do for you instead?'

'No, and now you can say goodbye Mary Green or is it Emily?'

Sophie raised her gun and Emily heard a trigger as shrapnel cut her hand causing a sharp pain. She landed awkwardly on the floor dazed and confused but as far as she could see she was still alive. She hardly dare look up and then slowly she raised her head and looked around the room. There was an eerie silence and she checked to see where Sophie was. At first, she couldn't see anything as the room seemed darker as a cloud came over the moon blocking all light from the window. As she looked closer, she noticed lying on the floor a body, it was Sophie's and it was motionless.

She shakily got to her feet and looked down and could see that Sophie was dead. She looked around the room puzzled and could at first see no one but then as she looked again she could see Susan her old friend who had worked in the kitchens from when Emily was a young girl at Herron Hall. She stood in front of her with a shooting gun in her hand.

'How?' Emily managed to say, her heart still beating quickly.

'Always keep the blasted thing.' Susan said looking more composed than she was feeling. 'What with the likes of me living on my own, you can never be too careful, it were me father's and besides,' she looked towards Sophie. 'After Herron Hall there's never been a night I've slept peacefully and I doubt if you have either, there was always some unfinished business waiting to show itself but now Emily you're past is finally behind you. Mary Green has long gone and you will always be Emily. You are a free woman to go forwards and never back.'

'Do you really think it's over?' Emily asked wanting to believe more than anything it was.

'Yes, Emily, your torment is finally over,' Susan said reassuringly and put her arms around her friend.

'May that be true, please may that be true,' Emily said.

'You can at last have the closure you've been searching for.'

Emily sighed. She looked at Susan and then at Sophie who lay motionless. Her dead body so still. Emily thought back to the death of her father. She closed her eyes and prayed that peace could at last be felt at the Hall. The Hall deserved that, it needed to be free of its past.

A breeze swept the room and a white feather blew through the open window. Emily knew instinctively that the feather belonged to that of her mother. Maybe the threads of the past had finally flown away. Herron Hall and all its secrets had now been set free just as she was.

To this day, Bella Green's presence can help still be felt at the Hall but nothing ever sinister or untoward has ever happened since.

Lightning Source UK Ltd.
Milton Keynes UK
UKHW021547150922
408915UK00005B/78